THE DARK SIDE OF SUPER

Matthew Siadak

Book Design and Illustrations by Laura Siadak

(https://www.fallenlights.net)

Edited by Damon Barret Roe

First edition: 2024

Paperback ISBN: 978-1-964375-00-7

Ebook ISBN: 978-1-964375-01-4

Author's Website: www.backwardsknight.com

Table of Contents

Content Notice

Notice of Content and Trigger Topics

Alcohol use
Swearing
Death
Blood and gore
Harsh language
Mind-control
Poisoning
Gun violence

To Laura, the other side of my story.
To Rho, who made this possible.
To my goat, may you ever find a story to tell.

HUSH, HUSH

H E COULDN'T—

Felix sucked in a breath, the air *whooshing* right back out through his barely parted lips. Repeating that, hand trembling as he placed it on his chest, he shook his head. He had to remember to breathe. Calm his mind down, even if it meant meditating in the club's bathroom.

Felix stared at the mirror hanging cock-eyed off the bathroom wall, deep within the club, its surface as cracked and fragmented as he felt. A myriad of faces—all his own, even if he didn't recognize himself—stared back from the distorted reflections in the broken mirror. Hollowed-out cheekbones, bloodshot eyes, a nervous tic at the corner of his mouth. Hair in disarray, swamped with sweat, his breath rattling in his chest. The hand there, nicked and bleeding from a few small, minor cuts. He focused on calming his heart by controlling his breathing, much the same way his sponsor taught him.

Breathe in. Hold.

Breathe out. Hold.

Wait.

With a chest empty of air and panic setting into his very bones, Felix waited to breathe, despite his heart pounding so hard, it drowned out the thumping music vibrating the walls. He held on, his head swimming. His fingers gripped the chipped and stained porcelain sink—in only slightly better shape than the mirror—his eyes watering with the need to breathe.

Just...breathe.

His sponsor's words echoed in his head, and yet he still waited to breathe. Counted another ten seconds out, an agonizing eternity between each one. Calm waves washed over him, threatened to draw him under, and only when he thought he might collapse to his knees did he draw in a breath. One that made his entire body shudder. Rancid club toilet stench crawled up his nose, into the depths of his lungs, but at least his heart no longer hammered against his ribs.

The sounds grew louder as the bathroom door opened, drawing his eyes over his shoulder, looking behind himself through the spider-webbed surface.

"Felix? Are you in here?" Marlie peeked in, her voice echoing around the grimy tiles that, somehow, still mostly clung to the walls. One or two more might have fallen off since the last time he counted them.

His mind itched to lose itself in the act of counting, but Marlie, sliding into the bathroom, distracted him. Her face appeared over his shoulder. For a moment, Felix looked two-headed in the mirror. That image made him laugh, bringing him back from that anxious precipice.

Marlie poked a finger roughly into the small of his back. "Hello? Ground control to Major Doofus? Time to wake up." Her nickname never failed to bring a smile to his face. Before he could open his mouth to answer, she linked her arm through his and dragged him away from the sink and toward the door.

As he started to protest, Marlie held up a finger. "Hush, hush. Hold that thought."

Felix closed his mouth, his eyes searching her face. Marlie merely smirked as she yanked the door open again.

Sound washed over him like a wave. As did the fountain of lights, multicolored and multidimensional, moving through a series of hypnotic, entrancing patterns that some club-goers stared at while under the effects of illicit substances. Stuff Felix tried to stay far, far away from.

Felix also stared at the lights, if only to be proud of his own handiwork. He loved seeing his algorithm in action, creating the seed of atmospheric data rendering to form the first series of lights each night. When the dance floor filled up, they morphed and changed based on the movement of the crowd. An ever-shifting sea of bodies generated an ever-changing kaleidoscope. One fed the other, and an eternal dance waited for those who would lose themselves in the light.

Any words he chewed on for Marlie lay trapped in his chest, confined by the oppressive, thrumming music. Even if he screamed—and, oh, how he wanted to scream—he knew the music would drown it out.

That might actually be preferable, Felix thought. He chewed on his lower lip again, coughing to clear his itching throat as Marlie led him through a crowd so dense, it practically held up the walls. The dancing bodies packed so firmly together nearly kept them caged away from the dance floor, but Marlie held no compunctions about diving right in. And apparently Felix didn't have a choice. As much as he might have wished to beg off dancing any more, her plans didn't leave room for his escape.

With fingers linked together, Marlie dragged Felix across the liminal threshold separating those who lost themselves to the music from those who had yet to leap. His throat, cracked and dry, beggared another cough. As Marlie pressed herself against him, hardly giving him a chance to move, the dance began.

With no idea what to do, he did what he did best—went with the flow. Like a stick in the river, twisting with the currents and undercurrents, Felix let the music carry him away.

He closed his eyes against the lights, against the press of Marlie, against the sauna-like heat that radiated from the surging crowd. The floor shimmied and swayed with the collective, beneath it, an ocean of concrete. The itch in his throat grew nigh unbearable. He knew how to sate it, but the thought of leaving this behind swelled like a wake within him. But the urge to find the balm for his throat grew untenable.

Somewhere between Marlie's frenetic movements, he managed to pantomime that he needed something to drink. Her hand slipped along his body, slick with sweat—his or hers, or both—as she smirked at him. She let go and faded into the throng of bodies, a skill he had never quite acquired. He watched her go if only for a moment. Her movements looked almost twisted, frantic, and wild in the strobing lights. Wild red hair flared as she turned this way and that, a stop-motion dance of beauty. Still, his burning throat drew him away. Felix bumbled across the dance floor, trying to let the music carry him through the flailing bodies and limbs until he escaped. Looking back, Felix barely avoided the urge to dive back in, to lose himself completely.

The further behind he left the dance floor, the sparser the bodies, and he soon made it to the edge of the bar. There, the music faded to the point he could hear himself think. The pain in his throat made him grimace. Standing on the tips of his toes, he spotted Sage at the other end of the bar. Wearing their usual grin—part smirk, part smolder—they had customers flocking to them. And not just for drinks.

As Felix wormed his way through the crowd, Sage lined up a series of shot glasses. Felix liked watching their work as they flipped and spun bottles, layering cocktail shots for the group of friends at the bar. Sage's movements were fluid, accentuated by their blond ponytail twirling around them. Like magic in motion, never failing to garner an audience.

Felix raised his hand, gaining Sage's attention once they were free. The way they poured drinks held nothing on their prowling saunter behind the bar, a beast in its den.

Sage shot him a wide grin. "Felix! What's the good word, baby bird?"

"Water." Felix paused for a moment. "Please." Another pause. "Whiskey, too." His throat hurt when he spoke, as if gravel lined his throat.

Sage frowned at him, their eyes pointedly looking at the token he wore on a bracelet. They started to speak but stopped as Felix raised his hand.

"It's not like that." He sighed when Sage refused to budge, staring him down, their gray eyes worried and searching. "Promise you, boo, it's not like that."

"Still, are you sure it's a good—"

"Give me a gods damned drink. *Right now.*" The words came harsher than Felix intended, but they jarred something loose in his throat, providing some relief. He coughed, glaring at Sage as they moved to get his drinks.

Shame unfurled inside him, but he squashed it down as he watched Sage. Their movements were more mechanical as they poured his drink quickly and snatched up a bottle of water, slamming them down in front of him. Before he could say something, anything, Sage disappeared to the other end of the bar without a backward glance.

I fucked up. That thought echoed through Felix's head. He hated himself more than ever for giving in, but with the damage done, with the drink in front of him? Might as well. He threw the whiskey back, the rotgut burning harsh in his throat, mixing sourly with the shame he felt from his demand to Sage.

Both curdled in his stomach.

"Don't worry about it none," Marlie whispered in his ear, her arms around his waist.

Felix closed his eyes, leaning back against her. His heart started to hammer again, and with the whiskey burning in his throat, Felix opened the water bottle and swigged it, desperate for a salve.

"What do you say we get out of here? See what else the town has to offer tonight?"

"I'm tired, Marlie." The burn of whiskey subsided beneath the cold-water chaser, but the rough itch inside his throat was building once more. A tickle to start, but he knew what it would grow into.

"I know, Felix, I know. But just keep your cool. Maybe we should get out of here, take a walk. Think that'd help? If nothing else, I have a proposition for you." Marlie spoke into the crook of his neck as her hands moved to press against his stomach, sneaking and snaking her way under his shirt, as she often did. Her touch helped calm him, but his heart still threatened to burst.

Felix swallowed a few more gulps of water, the alcohol acrid in his empty stomach, roiling straight into his blood. His skin warmed beneath her touch. He turned in her embrace, biting his lip.

Before he could vocalize the words rattling around inside him, they became barbed and lodged in his throat. Felix moved his hand to the nape of Marlie's neck, fingers gripping tight as he drew her in. She looked up at him, the rainbowed lights reflected in her eyes. Her normal green turned blue, pink, myriad colors painted against the sudden midnight of dilated irises that stared at him, waiting, wanting, devouring Felix with her gaze. The words burned in his throat more than the whiskey ever could, and he swallowed. Hard. Water bottle forgotten, Felix instead found sustenance with a press of his lips against hers, hardly having to search before she melted against him, her mouth pliant, matching his hunger.

Marlie broke the kiss first. "Tell me what you want." She coiled her body against his, wrapped her hands in his shirt, drawing him down to her height, their necks craned together. As if they were thick as thieves, she whispered again, fervently, as she bit his lip, "Tell me."

"*Get me out of here.*" Though the words scraped raw against Felix's vocal cords, the fog of whiskey settling over his mind lessened any anguish he might have otherwise felt. A part of him, somewhere beneath the liquored waves, screamed. It drowned in the flood, though, the last surges of its dying breath popping without notice. Burbled, really, so far inside of him, he could hardly hear himself think.

Marlie once more drew him by the hand, weaving through the club to fulfill his demand.

With his head spinning, Felix refused to look in Sage's direction for as long as he could. At the last moment, stealing a glance over his shoulder, he spotted them through the crowd, their face expressionless. That tugged a chord in Felix's heart, that their jovial way had dimmed, and why?

Because of me.

Felix pushed that down as the cold night air made its presence known the closer Marlie dragged him to the front entrance. Street light invaded the pervasive darkness of the lobby, beaten back only by the prismatic flashes ricocheting from the belly of the club.

Lifting a hand, Felix blocked out the harsh yet wan light casting the bouncers as tallow sentinels.

Marlie tugged, insistent, until they spilled into the cold street. Their sweat quickly cooled, making Felix feel clammy and cold. A visceral shiver convulsed through him as his breath clouded the air. Marlie wasted no time pressing against him, drawing his arms around her as they waltzed clumsily down the street. Felix wondered how they avoided tripping over one another and ending up sprawled out.

After a few steps, they found their old rhythm, and neither shied away from purposely bumping into one another, a promise of what's to come. Near misses that made both of them sputter with laughter as they wandered along the street. Felix had nowhere to go but he moved with haste, wanting to put as much distance as possible between himself and the club. Between himself and his shame.

After some time of meandering, Marlie spoke, standing on her tippy toes, pressing a kiss against his cheek which she followed with a lick. "Where are we going?"

Felix laughed again as he faced Marlie, which seemed to content her enough to hook her arm around his waist, sneaking under his own. His throat itched. He mourned the forgotten water bottle for a second, keeping his mouth shut before focusing on walking.

The late-night silence of the street welcomed them, a stark contrast to the rollicking hole-in-the-wall club. Her question roiled in his head.

The possibilities really were endless, but Felix dared not put voice to it yet. Where *did* he want to go?

"I don't know," he blurted, frowning as he shook his head. A wave of shame burned through the whiskey, the cold doing little to help either. "Maybe it's time to go home. I'm...tired."

Marlie pouted. "Not yet, no. It's barely past midnight. C'mon, Felix, we haven't had fun in ages. Real fun. Finding trouble. Hell, even making it." Her eyes sparkled. Now that they were out of the club, the dark green irises caught the streetlamps as they walked. She pleaded with him with that pout she knew rendered him powerless.

"I don't—I don't know about that." Felix swallowed against the pain simmering in his throat. Every bone in his body suddenly ached, and his eyelids felt like lead scraping over a bed of sand. He shook his head, which drew a whine from Marlie. "No, not tonight. Maybe tomorrow?" Felix offered, ignoring her whining. He continued walking. She caught up and pressed against him. Traffic started to pick up. This part of the city was always busy, with its flashing billboards and stores that never seemed to close. Ignoring the cold and Marlie's warmth, Felix pressed on.

That is, until Marlie stopped him and pointed. "Look at them, over there."

Felix followed with his gaze. A group of tourists stood gawking at the city, its surface-level splendor. Pointing at one of the larger towers, basking in the brilliance of the adverts' lights. Some with cameras flashing, others with phones out.

Easy marks.

Felix licked his lips.

Marlie smirked at him.

"It might not work, Marlie." Felix hesitated, not wanting to go further down that road. Not again.

"Come on. It'll be good for you. Live a little. Warm you up, and we can have a real talk somewhere nice and quiet like." Marlie grabbed his hand and moved, but Felix refused to follow, stopping her in her tracks, their arms stretched between them.

He shook his head. "No. We don't need their stuff. And we don't need to talk. I said no." And yet, Felix felt that familiar burn in his throat, the tension in his muscles.

Marlie let go and turned back toward him, her arms over her chest. "Come on. Just *talk* to them a little."

"No." Felix coughed again; the font of magma sticking to the inside of his throat making it hard to breathe, suffocating him. The sensation crawled over his skin. Sweat broke out over his brow. His stomach gurgled.

"When did you become so damn boring? I swear, Felix. I swear"—Marlie closed the distance again, her finger poking into his chest—"it was hard enough to get you out of the apartment. Been cooped up for so long." Each word punctuated by a poke. She drove him back, back, back. "Live a little. Give in. For old time's sake."

Felix shook his head and raised his hands to ward her off, but Marlie persisted.

"I don't see why—"

"Please, stop," Felix begged.

"Why? You could do it to Sage, you even used it on me to get out of the club. I'm trying to get you to open up. I need you to do this for me, babe." Marlie continued to press, driving him toward a ledge.

"I said no."

"When the fuck did you become such a little shit? This will be fun. Old Felix never would have said—"

Felix cut her off with a frustrated growl. "Just go. Leave me alone."

"No, Old Felix—"

Anger swelled, whiskey swirling, the world topsy-turvy. "Just—fuck—*fucking walk into traffic.*" Too late, Felix felt the itch in his throat subside. He blinked.

Marlie did too, before she turned around.

And walked.

ON THE STAGE

J ASPER HAD NO IDEA how many times his heart could skip a beat in one night. But at the current count of at least thirty-seven, not quite in a row, he knew he would lose count soon. Peeking through the stage curtains, almost blinded by the harsh lights beaming across the stage, he swallowed hard against the acrid, trembling nerves roiling through his stomach. Looking around and seeing no one paying him any mind, he reached into his jacket pocket for his flask. Warm whiskey soon splashed against the back of his throat, the burn of alcohol filtered from his taste buds and trickled lower, unknotting his coiled anxiety.

"Wake up, Jasper. You're on in five." Demi's voice crackled through the earpiece, the static drilling into his brain but his heart still swelling at the sound of her voice. Jasper took another long pull from the flask. Not that it had much left in it, but enough for two solid gulps to drain it. The liquid courage already churned within him.

"I'm ready." One hand on the mic as his other returned the dented and scratched flask to his inner jacket pocket where it slid against the silk lining. His fingers knew every scuff of the damn thing. How many nights had he watched his grandfather throw it at the television?

Shoving those memories into a well inside his mind, Jasper peered through the curtains again. He hiccupped from the cheap whiskey as he caught himself trying to count how many shadowed forms filled the seats beyond the purview of the stage lights.

He fidgeted as he ran through the routines he'd practiced over, and over, and over. And over again. By rote, he knew his way through his act forward and backward, and sometimes even blindfolded.

He chuckled at the thought. *Not really.* Though it felt as if he could, in the moment. But his nerves would never let him dare. Too much might go wrong, and he couldn't bear a return to the *before times,* when he was little more than a bumbling idiot obsessed with trying to do magic. Like just months prior, when he'd been laughed off the stage after flubbing one of the easiest card tricks that even the most novice of magicians could pull off—even his nephew, Rowan, who was, what, seven now? Maybe eight? That trick had been Rowan's pride and joy last Christmas, and Jasper had delighted in seeing the young boy take after him. Even though Rowan's mother, Lacie, hardly approved, Jasper hadn't cared. The scowl she'd shot Jasper, though?

Worth it. Totally worth it.

"Jasper, that's your cue."

Those words sparked something familiar inside him as his hand grasped the fraying edge of the curtain, waiting for a heartbeat, a second one. He suffered through the pause as his heart skipped again and counted a third beat before tugging on the thick red velvet. Pulling it aside, he was borne into the light, the warmth, the chaos of the stage. Sweat trickled down his back, like a cold finger along his spine. His eyes dilated despite the bright spotlights thrust at him, as if to pierce him with their beams.

Gazing out at the seated silhouettes, the servers walking through the crowd taking and delivering orders, Jasper cupped his hands to his mouth. "Hello! Is anyone there?" he called to the crowd of faceless beings in the darkness. Thinking of them that way lessened the fear that crept in even now that his heart pounded with the adrenaline of being out there, in the spotlight. On stage. "I can hear you all breathing." He paused before continuing, "It's kind of hot."

A few laughs escaped from the audience. *Good.*

"Listen, I don't know what you all expected to see tonight, but I'll let you in on a little secret: I'm going to blow your fucking mind with some real magic. Really *real,* I swear"—Jasper paused as the groans started, as someone out in the audience heckled him—"but let's start with a few simple 'oohs' and 'aahs' first, shall we?"

Before waiting for an answer, or another bait from the audience, he reached into the other side of his jacket and drew out his cloth sack, setting it on the table. The bag flopped, empty and flaccid.

"We're going to begin with some card tricks," Jasper started, withdrawing a deck of cards from his pocket. "Oh, wait, shit." Fumbling, he dropped the deck of cards, and kicked them beneath the table. He got on his hands and knees and crawled under the small table, collecting the cards as he went. A few more groans escaped from the audience, but he ignored them. Once he gathered the cards, he stood and pocketed them.

"That's the wrong deck, anyways. That's the one I use at the casino when the goons aren't paying attention." Another set of laughs, another spike of adrenaline making his skin tingle, charging him up for his performance. "Just let me reach into my magic bag here for a moment." Jasper held the bag up and reached into the apparent emptiness within.

"Now, these aren't my cards. These are for Demi." He withdrew a half-dozen roses, bound together, and frowned as he set them down. "Stand by, stand by. I swear I know what I'm doing." Reaching in again, he pulled out a large glass vase, full of water, and set it on the table, picked up the roses and put them in the vase. This earned him a few laughs, a few groans, and thankfully, the heckler remained silent.

"Sorry, sorry, like I said: these are for my dearest Demi, as an apology of sorts." Jasper sighed dramatically, reaching his hand back into the bag. More laughter followed as he shot the audience an *oops* sort of look.

"And what are you apologizing for now? What'd you do this time, Jasper?" Demi's voice filled his ear with concern. Worry. Dread. *"I swear—"* she started before another crackle of static cut her transmission short, the smell of burning electronics filling the air. He paused in his moment to palm the earpiece out, tossing it into the bag. He shot

a look toward Demi's booth, where he could see her frantic waving silhouetted through the window.

Breathing deeply, Jasper withdrew a few more things from the bag, setting each aside; a collection of handkerchiefs, rainbow and tied together, a few more decks of cards, an empty bird cage, and other magical props, all from within the same small, empty bag sitting atop the table. By now, even the heckler had quieted down and he heard the whispers building.

Which sent a shiver down his spine, to his toes, and back up once more. *Almost there.*

Jasper used his training to project his voice out into the auditorium, drawing every pair of eyes in the house to him. On him. "Are you ready for some real magic?" His heart raced with so many eyes trained on him, enthralled by his every move. His fingers itched with need as he reached into the bag one last time. He felt for the seam at the bottom, eyes closed. Jasper felt every thread in the cloth sack, even those that held it together. His fingers moved, twisted, turned, and he withdrew another deck of cards.

"Who wants to see a card trick? No? Too mundane? Check this one out, though. Promise." Card by card, one handed, Jasper moved through the entire deck. The audience started to groan. "What, that's not enough? How about this?"

And as he twisted each one through his fingers, they simply ceased to be.

The entire deck disappeared in thin air. Jasper held his empty hands up, turning them this way and that, and shrugged out of his jacket halfway, showing the cards were, simply put, gone.

"I could use some water. Pretty please?" He swiped his hand through sweaty locks, drawing them back from his face and tying them up with a hair band. As the waitress approached him with the pitcher of ice water, he pointed to her, then to her apron. "Before that, though, if you wouldn't mind retrieving my cards?"

The waitress shot him a confused look, flustered by the spotlight as it shone on her. She set the water down and reached into her apron, withdrawing the deck of playing cards. Turning it about, she showed it to the crowd first, then to Jasper.

"Oh, so this is where the cards went. Huh. I'll have to keep a better eye on them. Anyway, thanks for bringing them back!" Jasper winked at her as he used one hand to fan the deck of cards out once more. Taking the glass of water after she filled it, he drained it in one chug.

"Shall we proceed?" Silence, to start, came as an answer. He didn't have to wait long before people started shifting in their seats, whispering. He had their attention. Jasper grinned.

The rest of the evening blurred as he drew unwitting participants on stage. Drawing things out of their pockets that they didn't start the evening with. Trick after trick, applause after applause, Jasper drank it all in. He moved through his routine act by act, one after another, with little pause.

But it wasn't enough. It never was.

Jasper could see Demi up in the booth, where she sat in control of the lights and the sound system. She must have drawn open the blinds at some point to keep an eye on him. Even from this distance, he could see the concern, the worry, on her face. At one point, she mouthed, *what the fuck are you planning?*

Jasper just winked at her and dove back into his act. By this point, people had left the furthest booths and moved closer to the stage, filling the empty spots. He saw the glow of the spotlight in their eyes, all trained on him; an addictive, mesmerizing sensation. Jasper's hands moved lightning fast, trick after trick, drawing them in, inviting them closer.

"I have one last trick for you all. How's that sound?" Jasper held his hands up to a chorus of disappointed calls from the crowd. The person who heckled him earlier shouted out for more. Shaking his head, Jasper laughed and motioned to the audience to hush.

"Listen, one more magic trick. That'll have to do, you hear? Anyway, the next act, after me? You're just going to love Larry's lounge singing. I swear. Damn near cured me of my insomnia." Laughter broke out, loud and from multiple points in the room. A few good guffaws made Jasper grin wider than he had in some time. Probably since his last show.

Which means I need to go out with a bigger bang this time.

"I'm going to have to say 'Goodnight, Gracie' though, because I've already gone over my set time. I see Demi up there, waving madly at me because I am still blathering on. Telling me to cut, stop, whatever the *magic* word is. Everyone, say hi to Demi!" Jasper pointed to where she stood in the window of her booth. Everyone turned, looking around. He felt everyone *not* looking at him, and he closed his eyes.

Almost everyone. He felt Demi's glare. Jasper breathed in deeply, hard, until he felt as if he might burst. One hand reached for his bag on the table, into its mouth, and to the bottom seam. As he did so, he pictured the control room as clearly as he could.

First, Jasper pictured where Demi stood at the window, her perch from where she glared. The only set of eyes locked onto him. How many nights had he spent up there, with her, after his act? How many times had he walked through the back of the house, out past the bar, up the steps? The third one always creaked, like clockwork.

Not tonight. Jasper reached into his trusty little bag. Dug further, reaching to the impossibly far bottom of it. And beyond. Reaching into the fabric of the world itself, he found the seam wanting, waiting for him. An audible pop filled his ears. The sizzle and snap of smoke as a light popped on stage, drawing everyone's attention back to where he, decidedly, did not stand.

"What the fuck?" Demi shouted from right next to where he actually stood. Next to her.

Or where he would have stood, had vertigo not slammed into him, dropping him like an ungainly sack of bricks to the threadbare carpet prickly against his face.

"Jasper, what in the bleeding-bus-on-fire—" Demi shouted, straining for what mishmash of words to use next, and paused as he waved at her.

"Shhh, shh. Not yet." Jasper sat against her control station, catching his breath. As murmurs and calls drifted from the crowd, he leaped to his feet and waved and whistled down to them. All eyes turned to the control booth. To him, with shock and awe written clearly across every face. He felt the wonder in their gazes, almost like velvet.

A fresh wave of sweat broke over his skin as chills set in. Pain radiated from somewhere. No. Everywhere.

"Thank you all and may you all have a great night! I'll be back next Tuesday!" Jasper forced the words out through the PA system's microphone, fiery agony wracking his body. His skin flared into painful prickles shooting inward, along his spine, before radiating to the tips of his fingers and toes. "Well shit," he managed to whisper before a jolting cramp tormented his jaw shut.

"What the fuck—what the fuck did you do?" Demi hissed, her frustrated voice echoing through the speakers. She blanched, panicking as the audience started laughing, and turned her attention back to the sound panel, quickly cueing up music for the next performer. She slammed her mic's mute button and whirled on him. "What the shit was that? How? What? When? How? *What*?" With how wide her eyes were, Jasper half expected her pixie-cut blonde hair to be standing on end.

"Duh! Magic, silly girl." Jasper grinned as best he could, spreading his hands weakly, ignoring her stammering as he dry-heaved. *Oh shit, that hurts.* Nothing like when he had tried across the living room at home, though. Demi's gaze, barbed yet heavy with concern, followed his every movement, every twinge of pain.

"Shut the fucking fucked front door! What do you mean, are you one of—"

"No. I am most decidedly not." Jasper shook his head, closing his eyes for a moment, trying to will the pain away. "Just a little trick is all.

We can talk more later. I need to see a man about a duck." Not waiting for an answer—not that she could give one as the music ended, forcing her back to the microphone—Jasper stumbled toward the door. The pain started to lessen with every step he took, normalcy slowly filtered back into his body. Breathing remained difficult, and though his head spun, Jasper took the stairs two at a time down to the main floor.

Barely stopping once he reached the ground floor, Jasper stumbled straight toward the bar. His stomach churned as he took a seat and flagged down the bartender. He struggled to focus his eyes as another wave of pain surged through him, and he mumbled thanks as the bartender went to get his regular order, avoiding small talk. He reached for the drinks sloshed in front of him. Water, and a double whiskey sour. His hand wavered between the two, the other gripping his stomach as an aftershock shuddered through him.

"Breathe," Jasper told himself. For a few moments, maybe minutes, he did nothing but focus on his breathing. Nerves rattled, he decided on the water first, sipping at it as he tried to control his anxiety, waiting for his body to return to normal. Or as normal as he could guess with having done what he just did and pushing his limits. A part of him whispered in his sister's voice that he pushed *too far, too fast, too much*, but he ignored it. Jasper could still hardly believe he had managed such a huge jump. If not for the waves of agony, he might convince himself all of it was no more than a dream. After another long pull of water, he set it back down on the bar in favor of the cocktail. Lifting the tumbler to his mouth, a tendril of red weaving through the water drew his eyes. By the time he blinked, it spread and disappeared. Only then did he realize how very much his teeth hurt. Grimacing, he probed them with his tongue to see if any were loose before taking a careful sip of the whiskey sour. The burn spread through his entire mouth, stinging his gums before leaving a trail of fire down his throat.

"I see you've been practicing. While that *is* good, and I can see you've made solid progress, what's not good—and is actually downright stupid—is that you just flaunted it in front of a room full of people."

Despite the anger in the voice, the incredulous laugh in it made Jasper grin. "Hello to you too, Darlene." Jasper shot a look to his side, offering a smile, tight-lipped if only because he wasn't sure he wasn't still bleeding, and, well, she *did* chastise him. He saw the disappointment in her emerald gaze, and yet, she looked, what was that? Proud? Of him. He hated that he liked that, but what could he do? Not much more than to grin a little more.

"Just Darlie. Please. I told you before, I hate that extra 'ene.'" She scowled, as though the syllable soured in her mouth.

"Darlie it is, then. I'd ask what you thought of the show, but it sounds like you're my number one fan." Jasper continued grinning behind another pull from his drink. The stinging in his mouth abated, and the current charging through his body scattered.

"You could say that. I just wanted to make sure you were practicing nice and quiet like, and here I find that you're surpassing our every expectation. Don't make me get used to that." She smirked, running a finger through some of the condensation on the bar. Looking away, she hid her face behind a curtain of red hair. "What we talked about before. I need you to do a job for us, Jasper."

"Oh?" He sat up a little straighter, licking his lips, eager to hear more. After so many meetings, and teases of something on the horizon, he pictured it. A chance to prove himself, to find himself on the stage of a much larger production.

"Since you're doing so well, I need to see if you can put this, ah, particular skill to use. Good use, mind you, so don't fret." Her attention seemed split. Jasper looked around, trying to see what else had attracted it.

Jasper cleared his throat, furrowing his brows as his stomach threatened to creep into his esophagus. When that failed, he knocked back the rest of the whiskey sour, setting the empty tumbler down. Perhaps a little too hard. That worked, though, drawing Darlie's gaze back to him. Her words circled in his mind.

A job to do, a particular skill to use.

For a moment, with these clandestine meetings, a part of him worried. The rest of him wanted more.

Jasper leaned in closer. "What sort of job?"

"One that will pay you well. And will ensure that you're seen." Darlie gave him a knowing look at that, a grin, part smirk.

"Tell me more, tell me more." He leaned in closer yet, not trying to hide his eagerness. The look Darlie shot at him, though, as she stood, shaking her head, made his shoulders slump, sagging with disappointment.

"Maybe later. Looks like you have an even more adoring fan storming over. Here." Darlie tossed something at him.

Jasper nearly fumbled it in the air, barely catching it. "What's this for?" He inspected the phone, turning it over and over in his hand as if he could puzzle out the mystery. "I have one of these already, you know. You've texted me before—"

"And this one is for job-related details, and *only* job-related details. The less questions to start with, the better. I'll be in touch." Darlie pushed past Demi as she approached, quickly disappearing toward the entrance of the club. Jasper watched her go for a moment before he looked down at the sleek black phone in his hand again, his reflection staring back from the glossy screen.

"And just who was that?" Demi bristled with what he assumed was some sort of anger. Maybe concern. Maybe jealousy. Probably something in between all three. "And what the actual fuck was that?" She slammed her fist into his shoulder, making him wince, forcing his body to remember exactly how much pain it was in.

He tried to laugh it off. "Not the man about the duck I went to find, as it would seem, but the woman about a horse." He debated drinking from the water glass. He couldn't *see* the blood anymore, but he knew it was there. And he didn't want to see if more would dribble in. The pain outweighed the numbing effect of the alcohol running through him, and he wondered if a few more shots of whiskey might do the trick. Drown the pain in whiskey, and let future Jasper deal with it.

"I hate it when you get like this." Demi fought to stay mad at him, to not grin at his antics, which is exactly what he hoped for. Jasper knew her too well, and that the grin would wiggle free any moment all the same. "Seriously, though? You have to tell me how you did that." She hit his arm again, softer this time and with an open hand, the grin finally made its appearance.

He shot her a look. "I think you already know the answer."

"You tell me right now." Demi would have stomped her feet were she not sitting on the stool next to him.

"Okay, come a little closer." Jasper leaned in, and she followed, sitting as close as a pair of lovers. Her breath, hot on his neck. His face screwed up in pain, hidden in the crook of hers.

"Jasper..." she whispered, resting her hand against his chest. His heart skipped a beat again.

"A good magician never reveals his secrets, dear Demi."

She pulled away with an angry groan and a scowl. "Put that shit-eating grin away right now. Fuck you, you know? You can fool the rubes with that, but you fucking appeared right in my booth." This last part, at least, she hissed under her breath. "I'll say it again: what the actual fuck, Jasper?"

"Do you have your purse?" He scooted his barstool closer to hers.

"No, I left that locked in the booth. Why?" The look Demi shot him, her eyes narrowed. "Are you wanting to bum more—"

"No, no, stop for a second. Fuck, you asked." Jasper grunted in concentration, and another spike in pain.

"What does that have to do—Hey, what are you doing?" Demi hissed again as he reached into her jacket, as if he were going to draw her in for a kiss. And he could have. Gods know he wanted to. But this near, he saw the panic in her face, the way her eyes widened, her nostrils flared, drawing in quick, shallow breaths.

For all he hated to see the panic in her eyes, he enjoyed her gaze on him. Watching him. Others turned their heads too, watching them. Jasper smirked as he reached *further*, *farther*, picturing the booth she worked in night after night. He knew it like the back of his hand. How many after-set nights he had spent there, keeping her company?

Closing his eyes, Demi's warm breath commingling with his own, he *reached*. There, her purse, hanging where it always did on the back of the door. And there, in the pocket, her keys. His hands closed around the cold metal carabiner, drawing the weight of her keys into his palm. Heavy with all the tchotchkes she had on there—which everyone always teased her about, the way they made her jingle and jangle while walking. They could always hear her coming a mile away. Jasper imagined that noise as he withdrew his hand, using it as an anchor against the surging pain.

"Jasper?" Demi's voice, tinged with worry, came from just at his ear, but sounded like she sat a world away.

"Almost there." His words fell from numbed lips, which he licked. He tasted copper, warm and salty against his tongue.

"Jasper?"

Ignoring her and her panic, he pulled out her keys. They jingled all the way to the floor, falling with him as he collapsed into darkness.

Raindrops Fall

S TARING OUT OVER THE bay, Enid took a sip of her wine as she watched the chaotic waves, though they couldn't compare to the turmoil in her mind. "You know, the weatherman called for a sunny day, and the clouds are making a liar out of him." Hiding her smile behind another sip of wine, she turned her attention back to the person sitting across the small table, nose buried in her phone. Setting down her glass, Enid took her fork and continued picking and prodding at her food, taking small bites here and there while Tarly scrolled whatever digital distraction caught her attention.

Enid rolled her eyes. "Am I *that* boring, Tarly?" Cutting off another piece of steak, she savored the taste as it blossomed in her mouth.

"What? No. No. I'm trying to convince Felix that everything will be okay. He's been in a funk for the last week. Fuck, really, we all have, but we still need his help, so I need him to bounce back." Tarly shook her head and set her phone down, harder than she meant to given how she winced as it clunked against the wood.

"Did you go see him yet? That would do *wonders*, I bet." Enid quirked an eyebrow, smirking as she chewed on a bite of baked potato, savoring its salty, melting goodness.

Tarly shook her head vehemently, reaching for her phone again before thinking better of it. "No, no, I don't think *that* would help at all. No, not until I absolutely have to. If I have to, it'd have to be somewhere nice and quiet like. Maybe not at all. Better for everyone that way."

"With him out, and M still acting squirrely, I presume...?" Enid paused, a glare from Tarly serving as all the answer she needed. "That's going to throw some kinks into the works you've laid out in front of me, but"—Enid paused for effect, savoring another bite of her steak, another sip of her wine, dabbing at her mouth with her napkin—"I have no doubt you and yours have contingencies for contingencies, and back-up plans out the wazoo. Should I take it that we're proceeding as planned?"

"Yes. Can we count on you?" Tarly's words were punctuated by the first rain drop splattering against the window. She leaned over the table, her green eyes fierce beneath the bottle-black hair, which had already started fading, revealing the red hair below.

"Have I ever let you down?" Enid narrowed her eyes ever so slightly, daring her to say otherwise.

Tarly shook her head, held her hands up in a placating gesture. "No. But you are known to be, uh, a wild card sometimes. I need to know that you're going to be reliable. That we can rely on you."

Enid arced an eyebrow again. "What's with the sudden doubt?"

"This job, it's big. Like, real big. Biggest one yet." Tarly glanced at her phone as the screen lit up but ignored it.

"Listen, if you want my help, I'm here. I've never said no, keeps things quite lively for me that way. You can count on me one thousand percent. Tell me what needs doing, and I'll do it." Enid drained the last of her wine and set the glass down, looking askance at the raindrops peppering the window, obscuring the view of the outside world, turning it into a patterned kaleidoscope.

"Here's a phone. We'll get you details soon. There's still a few more threads to weave together, but it'll be soon. Be ready." Tarly didn't wait for an answer before she stood, setting the promised phone down in front of Enid. Tarly squeezed her shoulder and disappeared behind her, out of view, toward the front of the restaurant. Small, quaint, a hidden gem at the top of one of the hotels. Unlike most restaurants made to be sleek and modern, this one looked like an old cigar bar from sometime in the 50s.

Perfect for Enid to escape to. Or even have meetings in a place where she felt in control. More often than not, though? She came here to sit and brood, all while looking out over the world below.

Enid filled her wine glass from the decanter, staring at it as she did so. Her brows furrowed. Thunder rumbled in the distance, and worry built somewhere in the depths of her. Deeper than her stomach, a dark and hidden place, and yet she felt the effects all the same.

"Now's not the time, Enid," she muttered to herself, balling up the anxiety over Felix, and M being so withdrawn recently. Both of those gave her cause for concern, but she couldn't afford to be distracted. Not at this juncture.

And yet, as much as she shoved the worry outside of herself, the rain grew heavier, thunder rumbled closer, she found she couldn't dismiss all of her emotions. A thread of them remained, no matter how hard she tried to cut herself free.

Chewing on her lip in contemplation, Enid picked up the phone Tarly left and swapped it for the one in her pocket. She thumbed through the notifications waiting for her, most of it spam or people whose existence she had no intention of acknowledging. One message concerned her, about her latest paycheck being placed on hold.

Fuck. That's not good. It should've cleared yesterday. Enid glanced at the door, as if she could will Tarly back to cover the bill. Panic set in as Enid opened her banking app and saw the balance. Not enough to cover the bill they'd racked up. For a moment, she thought about calling Tarly with the other phone, but quickly discarded that idea. *Wouldn't be the first time, but man, I love this restaurant.* She threw those emotions right out the window with her anxiety, leaving her calm, collected.

Enid resumed thumbing her way through her notifications, mostly useless junk, before she managed to get to her texts. Nothing of importance there, so she opened her contacts, searching for a name.

After a few moments of hesitation, she started a new message.

Hey, J. We haven't spoken in a bit. I know you did a show recently. How'd that go? Has Darlie met up with you yet?

Enid typed, thumbs flying across the screen, typing it all out without sparing a glance at the phone, instead, searching for the waiter. Cursing herself for not taking the opportunity to ask Tarly for an update on Jasper when she had it. After a few moments of hesitation, she dropped her phone unceremoniously on the table, leaving the message unsent. Thunder rumbled again as she tamped down her worry, shoving it down, away, out of body. Out of mind.

Returning her attention to her food, she pushed around the last few bites on her plate. With no real appetite remaining, Enid instead sipped at her wine. Sighing as the taste of it curdled against her tongue. Setting the glass down, Enid closed her eyes and breathed deep. In, hold. Out, hold. She repeated that, fighting against the roiling anxiety and worry in her stomach, realizing she hadn't stamped them out at all. As she sought to calm herself, lightning flared, thundered, shook the building as it hit something close.

Perhaps too close.

The darkness behind her eyelids deepened as she breathed a few more times. A small smile played over her lips as she peeked one eye open and confirmed the restaurant sat without power, dark but for emergency lights. She closed her eyes again and waited. Enid knew what happened next. She waved her waiter down.

Like clockwork, he wandered over to her table. "Ma'am, I'm sorry, but it appears the power has gone out." Enid glanced at his gilded nametag before putting a little worry and concern on her face as Chet continued speaking. "Our systems have gone down, and the machines take some time to reboot once the power kicks back on. If I could get you anything else while you wait...?" His narrow face remained calm, placid, his tone jovial, but Enid noticed the look in his eyes. Furtive. Worried.

Whether he expected her to launch into a tirade, or something else, Enid couldn't be certain. "You know what? I actually think I'm done and ready to go." She paused as Chet narrowed his own eyes, batting her own eyelashes in return. "Why don't you bring me my check anyway? You can take my card details down and fill out one of those forms, you know? With the click-clack thing? An imprint machine, I think it's called? I have a very important meeting I need to attend that I simply cannot be late for." Another lighting flash, nowhere near as close, as Enid remained calm. Breathed through the words falling easily out of her mouth.

"Are you sure? We have a lovely dessert made special by the chef, or I could bring you more wine?" Chet pushed.

Enid smiled calmly as the storm raged against the restaurant's windows. "I don't think so. I will give you my card details, and you will take them, and a sizable tip." Chet opened his mouth, but she cut him off. "And I won't have to ask for a manager, will I? Hmmm?" Enid's voice took on a slight edge to it, her lips curling into something resembling a smile. A sharp one. She *tsk*ed a few times as Chet turned and walked away.

He quickly returned with the credit-card imprint machine. Enid searched through her purse for her wallet, and then through the cards. She pulled out the small black rectangle whose surface remained unmarred but for the small chip. It made a metallic clink as she sat it on his tray.

"Thank you, ma'am. I'll fill this out. I apologize for pushing the issue." Chet's eyes widened almost imperceptibly as he studied the card. He tried to hide it, but Enid noticed it. Counted on it. Never mind that the card, long since reported stolen and deactivated, wouldn't do him any good. Not until the power came back on, at least.

Chet ran it through the clunky machine, filled out the paperwork, and handed it over to her. She felt his gaze as she took the pen and dotted out a tip closer to half the bill than anything else, before signing with a flourish.

"There, and just a little extra for the troubles today, yes?" Enid offered with a generous grin as she stood from the table, grabbing her phone. Leaving Chet behind, she unlocked her phone with a press of her thumb. Her text to Jasper waited. With the storm washing away any of her concerns or worries, she read the text two or three times before deleting it. She made her way past those also looking for their checks, left to deal with the power outage.

Enid ignored all of them and strode with purpose. Other than the people talking, the place sat eerily silent, what without the whirr of electronics. Almost peaceful, except for the arguments starting of other people also wanting to leave and the occasional rumble of thunder. She ducked out, away from that, into the silence outside. Her heels clacked against the marbled-tile floor.

At first, thinking about taking the elevators, Enid sighed when the button remained as dark as the lobby outside the restaurant. "Right. About that," she muttered to herself. Looking around, she spied the door to the stairwell, tucked away in a corner as if its mere presence might offend someone. Ducking that way, Enid made a mental note that this restaurant was off of her list for now as she escaped beyond the heavy door. She paused to take her heels off before descending the stairs.

In the tomb-like, cinder block stairwell, with creaks and distant rumbles echoing, she paused to look out one of the windows. Pulling away from there, Enid descended to the street. After a few floors, others started to filter in, until the crowd swallowed her whole and she no longer had to think about much except moving with the flow of people leaving the building.

Which let thoughts of Jasper creep back in. With them came a little worry, to start. By the time she reached the street level and stepped outside, no remnants of the storm remained in the sky, which perfectly suited her. Leaning against the nearest wall, she put her shoes back on with one hand as the other typed out another text.

Jasper. Hope you managed the spotlight with your usual aplomb. She stared at the words on the screen for a moment before slipping into the stream of passers-by. As she stepped out of the signal dead-zone of the stairwell, her phone chirruped angrily.

Ignoring the incoming notifications as they popped up, she chewed on her lip and hit send before immediately turning off the screen. On the off-chance Jasper replied, she kept her phone in her hand. She pulled the hood of her peacoat over her head against the light and sprinkling rain that persisted through the sun. People crowded the streets as chaos settled in beneath the now-darkened signs usually lit up with a visual cacophony of neon and LED lights. The clamor of pedestrians reached a crescendo, though, as horns started blaring, impatient people attempting to navigate the intersection with no lights to guide traffic.

After a few moments, the shrill, ear-piercing sound of a cop's whistle sounded as he waded into the mess with his hands up, trying to find a way to stem the tide of angry drivers.

Enid frowned, her eyebrows furrowing as she observed the chaos of the block without power. Wondered, for a moment, how far it might have spread.

"I guess a cab's out of the question," Enid muttered, biting her lip. "Fuck." She wondered if the subway suffered the same fate. "Had to go and dine-and-dash, like a stupid bitch." Enid drew a deep breath, pulling her emotions in and up, letting the anger at herself blossom in the center of her chest. The rain drops around her lessened, at least. She knew that, depending on how or where the lightning had struck, there was little to no guessing when the power might come back. Especially if the utility workers couldn't get through the mess of traffic.

Enid went back to the contacts in her phone, her thumb hovering over Jasper's name. She pressed the button, watched the phone start dialing, heard the ringing. Her mind caught up with her and she pressed the hang-up button before the call completed the connection.

She almost dropped the phone as it started vibrating in her hand, an insistent tug at her attention. She swallowed hard at the name flaring on the screen before answering. "Jasper, it's about damn time—"

A feminine voice rattled off through the phone. "No, this isn't Jasper, please, wait. Please. I haven't been able to reach anyone else."

"Who is this? Why do you have his phone? Where's Jasper?" Enid's voice fell low, and she surprised herself with the level of growl in it. A myriad of different scenarios played out in her head, none of which helped her feel any better. Enid placed a hand over her chest, her heart tightening with worry.

"He hurt himself the other night, at his show. He's been in the ER the last few days; I've been with him. I wasn't able to reach anyone, didn't know who to try calling. I didn't know his phone passcode, but you called. I could finally do something, anything. Your number popped up and I called back!" The person on the phone breathed heavily before she continued. "I don't know what he did, how he did it—"

"Stop right there. This isn't the time, nor the place, nor the way in which I want to have a conversation like *that*." Enid paused and ducked into the mouth of an alley; the receding rain having driven away most of the stench of the city. Petrichor bloomed in the air. She drew a deep breath. "First things first, breathe. There. Calm. Okay? Let's start with this next: what's your name?"

"Demi."

"Okay, Demi. I'm—"

"Enid. The phone showed your name when you texted," Demi continued with a manic sort of edge to her words.

Enid bit her tongue at the interruption and forced herself to breathe for a moment. "Second thing, I get it: you're all out of sorts, it's been a rough few days and hasn't been easy by any means. I get it, but please, please, do not interrupt me." Enid sighed, pressing her finger and thumb against the bridge of her nose as she closed her eyes.

"Okay, I'm just worried, he's not doing good." Demi's voice trembled, the noise of which drove another spike of anxiety through Enid, straight into the meaty part of her brain, ricocheting straight to her heart.

"Where are you two? Where's my brother?" She peeked one eye open to look at the sky.

"Oh my, oh, you're his sister. I'm so sorry; I wish I could've called sooner."

"Okay, it's okay. Breathe. Please, where are you? Where is Jasper?" Enid did her best not to scream into the phone to get information.

"Downtown. Hope Haven Community Hospital. Room 1408. Somehow, he managed a private one." Demi let out a hiccupping laugh.

"One moment." Enid drew her phone away from her ear, opened the map app, and searched. Cell traffic further burdened by the power outage made it slow. "Hold that thought," Enid said as she heard Demi saying something through the phone. "I'm not far, and while there's no way I'm catching a cab in this mess, I'll be there as soon as I can." Enid ended the call midway through Demi saying something. "Fuck." Frozen in a moment of indecisiveness, she decided to flick open her texts. She scrolled through until she found Tarly's number.

Jasper's hurt. Sounds bad. Might have to find a plan B there too. Halfway through finding something to doom scroll on as she walked, Enid's phone vibrating surprised her.

(Tarly) We know.

(E.) …You could have told me.

(Tarly) Darlie considered it a need-to-know.

(E.) Uh, that's fucked. Jasper's my brother, how is that NOT need to know?!

(Tarly) Orders came from on high. I'm sorry.

(E.) First Felix, and now Jasper. You're going to run out of contingencies soon.

(Tarly) Enid, don't worry. Everything is going according to plan.

(E.) Wake up and smell the shitshow.
(Tarly) We have this under control. All going to plan.
(E.) WHOSE PLAN HURT MY BROTHER?!
(Tarly) We'll talk later. I promise.

Swallowing her concern and worry not only for Jasper, but for herself as well, Enid glared at the phone. "Screw you too." She saw the rictus of her snarl reflected in the darkened screen. Her heart hammered, her breath heavy in her stomach. Knowing full well Tarly would ignore any more messages she sent, she closed that conversation and opened another.

Nikhail. Problem. Need you at HHCH right fucking now. Yesterday even. Room 1408, I'll get everything situated. Enid hit send and started walking again. For half a moment, she wondered if she shouldn't give Nikhail a call, but quickly dismissed that idea. That'd end her hope to get his attention before it ever began. She sighed and walked faster, fishing out her earbuds to drown the world out with some Preisner, something that never failed to calm her nerves. She followed the directions of the GPS on her phone, letting it guide her as the skies stormed once more.

Along her walk, the chaos from the power outage grew. Enough that those who didn't have to be out on the streets weren't, which meant she didn't have to struggle through crowds of people. While the power outage ended after a few blocks, the chaos stretched further, radiating from the locus. This let her make better time than she anticipated. What with the reduced foot traffic and cars at a standstill even if they had a green light, Enid darted across the street, ignoring the angry honking.

The hospital, its façade drab and depressing, took up a good chunk of a city block itself. Parts of it sprawled outward, reaching toward other buildings with skywalks crisscrossing the sky itself, blotting out the sun. Not unlike a giant spider's web, tying everything to the hospital.

Enid stood in the shadow of one such skywalk, her gaze lowering to the hospital entrance. She could practically smell the antiseptic sterility already, a scent that held no good associations for anyone. She hated it, steeled herself against it as she mounted the short flight of steps up and grabbed a surgical mask over from the '*Cover up if you have a cough!*' station. *That'll help with the smell, at least.* Enid didn't let herself stop, as much as her mind recoiled from the looming lobby.

Her momentum carried her past the rotating door. As much as she wanted to complete the rotation and eject herself back out onto the street, she couldn't. *Jasper.*

As Enid expected, she shuddered from the overwhelming hospital smell, a pressure already building behind her eyes, in her sinuses. Checking her phone, she frowned at the lack of notifications from Nikhail. Before making her way to the elevator, she stopped in the coffee shop, picking through the cards in her wallet. A pang of remorse hit her, seeing the black card and, for the briefest of moments, she felt bad for Chet. She shoved that down, though, and stepped up to the counter. A yawn hit Enid out of nowhere, and she held up her hand as the barista stepped up, catching her in the middle of it.

"Two coffees. Three. All heavy on the sugar and cream. A couple of extra shots, too, in one of them. You know what, make it four." Barely even looking at the barista, she swiped her own credit card through the machine, only remembering to breathe when the transaction went through without issue. No alarms blared, which she half expected despite the fact that it wouldn't have made sense. Her brain, her worst enemy.

Stepping to the side, filled with nervous energy, she looked out the inner window of the coffee shop back to the lobby, looking for Nikhail with a hopeful twinge in her chest. Again, against all reason, she hoped that she might spot him, that he'd miraculously show up without having answered.

Enid hoped to cut off the sense of dread growing within her heart before it had a chance to change her mind. She had to tell herself contacting Nikhail was for the best.

The barista appearing in her periphery drew Enid back out of her own mind. "Thanks," she offered with a distracted smile as the barista set the drinks down. She picked one up to sip at, holding the carrier in her other hand. The coffee, just short of scalding, drove away the chill inside of her. Happy for that, at least, she strode to the elevator. Pressed the button, waited, heard the ding, stepped into the elevator.

Enid stepped to the back, leaning on the paneling straight out of the 70s. She closed her eyes and tilted her head against the wall, the hood of her coat staving off the harsh, white overhead lights. As the elevator rumbled beneath her feet and dinged with every passing floor, Enid waited. Even there, that smell continued to assault her. Nausea settled heavily on her stomach, and she wondered if her face had actually turned green around the gills yet.

As the elevator climbed slowly, Enid recounted the chaos of the day. Especially her actions, once again lamenting that she had likely burned a bridge at her favorite restaurant. How long until they forgot about her? Would they? She focused on those questions instead of the undercurrent of anxiety for Jasper, and herself, and the mess they found themselves embroiled within. All of this business, the pushing of Jasper to do more and more, and now he's in the hospital?

Enid realized she was grinding her teeth in anger and stopped before the emotion boiled over and out of her. She closed her eyes and forced herself to breathe.

On the twelfth ding, she opened her eyes and pushed off of the wall of the elevator, stepping out into a hallway that looked the same in both directions. Nurses milled to and fro, some more frantic than others, accompanied by the low hum of beeps, thrums, and whispers. No one paid her any mind, which suited her just fine.

"Where are you, Jasper?" Enid checked the placards indicating room numbers and directions. There. Room 1408. At the end of one of the hallways. Enid headed that way, finding the door ajar. She raised her hand to knock just as the door was yanked open.

"Do you know anything yet?" half snarled a distraught woman, short blonde hair in disarray.

"Whoa there, whoa. You must be Demi, right? Enid. We spoke earlier on the phone? Y'know?" She would've held her hands up, and almost did, which would've resulted in coffee everywhere.

Any fight in Demi bled away, leaving her wilted. "Oh. I thought you were the nurse, or one of the useless doctors."

"Here. Coffee. I figured you might need something better than the swill this place offered." Enid handed over the carrier. "One for Jasper, too. Is he awake?"

"Oh, what? Yes, yes. Please. I need to get my heart going." Demi, both coffees in hand, nudged the door back open, giving Enid room to step around her.

She passed through the barrier of antiseptic-smell that grew stronger between the hallway and the room. The television played silently, casting odd shadows against the privacy curtain drawn halfway.

"Jasper?" Enid paused, uncertain still.

"Enid? Is that you?" Jasper, half-slurring his words. Obviously exhausted but somehow still chock full of his ineffable energy. He almost sounded happy.

"The one and only." Enid put on the bravest smile she could, finally peeking around the curtain. The sight that greeted her threatened to bring back memories. Way, way too many memories, and she worked quickly to shut those down. Focused on the here and now, much the way her therapist taught her.

"You're looking like a drowned rat," Jasper said, the grin on his face twisting in pain.

"Better than looking like whatever you are. I'm pretty sure scientists are still hard at work trying to classify what sort of natural disaster, man-made extinction event, and sheer stupidity all commingled into one fleshy meat-sack could yield such a shitshow, kiddo." Enid smiled through the words, though, tears coming unbidden to her eyes as she drew a chair closer and sat next to the bed. Jasper looked rough, thoroughly poked and prodded with wires and tubes every which way. But at least he laughed.

That made her smile, which also made her cry.

Jasper tried to smile again. "Don't cry, Nini. It's nothing serious."

"Don't bullshit a bullshitter, Jazz. You never could pull one over on your bigger sister." She leaned in closer, reaching for his hand, gave it a careful squeeze and didn't let go. "What happened?"

"He's a dumb blasted fucking idiot," Demi chimed in.

Enid shot her a glare, eyes narrowed. "Listen, you can call him whatever you want when I'm not here, but—"

"Cool your jets, Nini. Demi's good people, I promise. She's not wrong. I pushed myself too hard." Jasper looked away from her, anywhere but at her.

Enid knew that look. "What the fuck did you do, Jasper?"

He grinned again, wincing in pain. "I did it."

"How far?" Enid blinked, glancing furtively at Demi.

"Don't worry, she knows." He looked away again, and it took all Enid had to not swat him.

"How far?" she pressed, biting her lip.

"About ninety feet." Jasper beamed.

She nearly fell out of her chair. "Shut your mouth! What the fuck, man?"

"I've been practicing. I didn't want to goof up on the big day." The smile faltered a little.

Enid leaned in closer, reaching to push a sweat-slicked lock of hair away from Jasper's face. "And what got you in here? Teleport out the other side of a building?"

"Nothing like that," he spoke quietly, just like he always did when he knew he was in trouble.

"The doctor said they've never seen such a case of the bends, that deep-sea diver sickness. Not like this, when it doesn't respond to any of the normal treatments," Demi said, moving to the other side of the bed, trapping Jasper between them.

Enid arched one fine eyebrow, looking between the two of them. "I see."

"Nini. Enid." Jasper finally looked at her again as he spoke. "I'm fine. I swear."

"One, you didn't tell me you had a girlfriend," Enid said, catching him off guard. The blush on Demi's face spoke to that, at least. "And two, I'll have to contact Tarly and Darlie. There's no way you can be part of this, not if you risk dying. I won't allow it." Shaking her head again, she reached for her phone.

Demi shot Enid a silent thank you but Jasper's hand moved like a viper, stopping Enid from reaching her pocket.

"Listen. I was dumb, I'll be fine. The doctor said so," Jasper pleaded as he tried to leverage his grasp on her to sit up.

"Not quite, you damn dingus," Demi said, sighing. "They said you'd be fine *if* they can find a treatment that works. Long term."

"Nini can call Nik—"

"Already on that. No answer yet. And even so, I'm not going to get you fixed up only to turn around and risk you again." Enid narrowed her eyes but didn't wrench her hand free. Not with the danger of yanking Jasper about roughly, risking his IV.

"There's no problem here, Enid. I won't be dumb about it this time."

She glared at him. "And you'll keep your stunts to a more controlled experiment?"

"As much as I can, what with this *power outage* that rocked the city today. It's been all over the news." His words came with a knowing look. "Anyway, I'm a grown-ass man. I told Darlie I'm in, and I am in. That's that." He let go of her hand and rolled over.

Enid opened her mouth, but the look on Demi's face—that this woman would rather be anywhere else and yet would never leave Jasper as the siblings squabbled—made her close it with a snap of her teeth.

"Fine." She sighed. "Once I hear from Nikhail, I'll let him know where to go. Just, just be careful, okay?" Enid stood and squeezed Jasper's shoulder. "Take care of him, okay?" This she shot to Demi, who was already nodding.

Nodding herself, Enid left. As she walked through the hallway, thinking of a way she could reach out to Darlie or even Tarly, get this sorted out, get Jasper off the roster. Without thinking twice, she walked past the elevator and ducked into the stairwell.

Worry built in her stomach, anxiety tightened her chest, her mouth felt dry. *Stupid Jasper. Stupid, stupid Jazz.* Those words, and worse, ran through her mind as she headed down the stairs. Breathing deeply, she centered herself as best she could, the way her therapist had taught her, until she could escape the hospital altogether.

Outside, the sky opened up as Enid let her coiled emotions flood out of her. Lightning flashed, thunder cracked. She watched raindrops fall, washing away her emotions into the storm, sighing as she emptied herself for peace and quiet.

MAN IN THE MIRROR

D AYS LIKE TODAY DRIVE home the feeling that I no longer know who I am. Not anymore, and not for some time. I cannot remember the last time I felt like myself, whole and connected to the world at large. Everything—sounds, scents, sights—comes in through a filter. Through a haze of the unknown, or maybe even the unknowable.

Sitting on the bus, I am pretty sure I have long since missed my stop. But where was my stop? Maybe it missed me. I could not be bothered to stand up and leave. Instead, I watched the doors close, locking me into a repeating circuit through the city. I did not know where it went after I usually got off. I rarely ever needed to know.

I decided, by inaction, to change that today.

The bus driver glared at me a few times from his mirror, until I stopped paying attention and stared out the window, watching as the city passed me by—or as I passed it. I could lose myself in the illusion of being stationary while the world chugged along without me. And yet, the weight of those blue eyes above that slightly crooked nose continued to watch me. With concern? Contempt? I could not tell. Those eyes were all I could see of the driver, whose countenance lived solely in the mirror. I tore my own gaze away and watched the skyline once more.

It was only when we passed an underpass, when concrete blotted out the sun, that I saw a stranger, a man in the mirror staring back at me in my reflection. Sitting in my seat, wearing my clothes, my face obscured by some crude symbols or words scratched into the window. Part of my hair, in the back, stuck up stubbornly. A dirty-blond cowlick, one that had driven me mad over the last few days. I smoothed it down as best I could over a bald spot that seemed new. I sighed, watching my supposed self overlaid on the ever-changing cityscape. A layer on top of a layer, the city a backdrop to me, where I sat unmoving, whirring along with the lumbering bus.

My phone rang in my pocket as I focused on just breathing, just being. I set it on the empty seat next to me and ignored it. *I don't want to work today. Or ever again.* I drew a deep breath and held it, counted to four, and let it go again. Rinse and repeat. So it goes, though I could still feel the phantom vibrations in my pants, against my leg. One glance toward my phone, with its screen still dark, told me all I needed to know. Whoever had been insistent in reaching me gave up.

For now, at least. I grimaced because I knew. "That will not last forever," I vocalized the rest of the thought before shaking my head. My voice seemed distant, alien and strange to my own ears. I coughed, clearing my throat, which garnered another glare from the bus driver. I did not look, did not need to, to feel the pointed stare. I looked around at the empty seats surrounding me, and the ones surrounding those, and on and on.

How long have I been here by myself?

I tried to recall but found the memories fleeting, ephemeral in my grasp, my mind all over the place. As short-lived as the ever-changing shape of the skyline.

Another pattern of vibrations drew my attention back to the phone. I reached for it. My hand stopped halfway there, and I stared. A ring on my finger caught the sickly light filtering through the window. Daylight, not quite faded, struggled to pass through the sticky, shaded window of the rattling, old bus. Diminished that much further for it by the time it glinted erratically, caught in the scratches and dings in my ring.

I turned my hand over, first looking at the well-worn lines there. I searched for the scar, the faint line that served as a stern reminder of who I was, once upon a time. And yet, every passing year, it grew that much fainter, making it harder to find. Whenever I looked for it anymore, I had to trace that patch of skin with my thumb to find it. No matter what, that scar was with me for life. I could almost hear my father's voice. Would have, if I let myself, if I did not immediately quash those thoughts. Those feelings. No point in remembering those. Had I pushed them down so far, though, that the scar disappeared? I remembered the slicing shard of glass, the blood painting the floor.

But not much else.

Or had the physical memory of the wound simply faded over time, the way the more stubborn memories refused to? I studied my hand as if I could tell my own fortune, but nothing became more apparent than the bus had stopped. Noticeably stopped. My body rocked, as if commiserating a distinct lack of motion, and I forgot about my scar.

Risking a glance, I found the bus driver's seat empty. Beyond the windshield, the skyline had been replaced with a drab, squat building the color of my grandmother's mashed potatoes. My stomach turned, wanting nothing more than the almost-relaxing sway of the bus. The bright lights of the bus depot's sign replaced the sunlight, blues and whites and reds drilling into the innards of the bus. Back at the station.

I sat very still, quiet, afraid to even do more than breathe. My phone vibrated again. I ignored it.

Fear crept into my stomach from somewhere dark, driving a chill through me as my heart raced to compensate. Where had the driver gone? Was he calling the police? Did he know? I bit down on my lip as I checked outside, toward the rear of the bus as if that might answer my burning questions. No lights, sirens, or anything concerning to be seen. And yet my heart continued racing, hammering against my ribs. My phone vibrated again, insistent for my attention. I ignored it, remaining still in my seat, looking out the back window, then the front.

"Shift change. Fred said you were going to be in here. All nice and quiet like." The words and the voice that spoke them did so from out of nowhere. Then a head sporting a bus company hat peeked over the handrails at the door. A body followed as a new driver took her seat. I blinked a few times before her words made sense. I had ridden the bus long enough that Fred brought us back for another driver to take over.

I bit my lip, one fingernail scratching at the well-worn fabric of the seat. "I am sorry, I just—"

"Listen, it's okay. You're okay. I know what it's like. When you just need a day to not do anything, to go absolutely nowhere and everywhere all at once. Is that right?" The look she gave me, it said a lot. For a moment, I let myself believe that maybe she *did* know. That she could understand.

I nodded. "Do I owe more?" My voice came out haggard, a quiet whisper that managed to fill the empty, silent bus.

"Not if you're willing to sit a little closer. Talk and keep me company during my drive. Night shift always tends to run slow on my route, so having someone to talk to will make all the difference." She shot me a tired smile, a hopeful look.

"Okay." I looked at my phone and considered leaving it there. I decided against it, sighing. Picked it up and shoved it back in my pocket before making my way to the front of the bus, looking out each window as I went as if some other landscape might greet me than the bus depot.

But no. The world remained static.

"I'm Charlie." The bus driver offered, her green eyes staring at me from where Fred's blues had earlier.

"I am..." I trailed off, another wave of uncertainty hitting me, walloping me right in the face. *Who am I?* That question plagued me today. I shook my head, clearing my throat.

"Where are you headed, after all this?" Charlie watched me in the mirror as I took a seat nearby, a curious look on her face. My silence drew that into a worried look.

Her question lingered in the air, and before her frown could grow too much more, I answered, "Home?" My voice betrayed me as it came out in a question I did not mean to ask. This confused me. *When did I start sounding so old?* I closed my eyes and leaned into the seat, a wave of vertigo swimming through my head. "I just want to go...home."

Charlie kept true to her word and kept speaking. "I see. I get that too. What did you skip out on today?"

I relaxed a little into the seat, my fingers drumming against my leg. "Work. I guess you can call it that."

"Work?" She guffawed. "Aren't you, you know, a bit late for that? 9-to-5s usually are in the morning, buddy."

My brows furrowed. "Not that sort of work." I resisted the urge to check my phone as it vibrated again, a pulsing, insistent warble against my leg, tip-tapping up and down until I placed my hand on it and inhaled deeply. Held it, counted, let it go, trying to find myself in the quagmire of doubt and anxiety filling my chest, like a gnarled tree blotting out the sun. "No. I have a loose schedule and can come and go as we—*I*—need to."

"That sounds like a great life to live. Well, after that of driving a bus," Charlie said, smirking as she gazed at me through the mirror. "Can't beat this, owning the road and a set path day in, day out." With that, she twisted the key in the ignition, pressing past mechanical complaints before the engine roared awake, lurching into motion.

The station quickly fell away, replaced by the shifting city once more. A darker shade of it, to be certain, the sun disappearing behind the buildings, reflecting its dying gasps of light in the windows of the city, casting blood-red specks of light. Those, too, began to fade, the red shifting to a faint purple, darkening like a vivid bruise, until night came full-on black.

Charlie kept speaking, her words never quite reaching the central part of my brain. I found myself answering with vague noises, sometimes affirmative, sometimes noncommittal. I did not fully process her words, but my gaze kept going back to the mirror, back to what I could see of her face. Those green eyes, that slight, knowing look. A smirk? Decidedly less smug, though. Maybe. I rubbed my hand over my face.

My stomach gurgled. Whether from subsisting on little more than the fumes of the bus, or from anxiety that Charlie looked familiar, leaving me to wonder where I had seen her. It wasn't like I often rode the bus that late.

Did I?

I didn't know. I didn't know myself, not anymore. And that scared me.

"Don't worry your head off none." Charlie's words brought me back to the here and now. I could not drag my gaze away from my own reflection, though. There, at the front of the bus, the window had even more of its surface worn away, leaving me staring at a tattered visage of myself.

I laughed. I felt something start to give, to melt, to weaken, and the laugh kept coming. Part from fatigue, and part from the mental strain, I felt myself ready to break one way or the other. I put my hand over my mouth to try to stop it. To no avail.

Charlie laughed, too, a mirror of my own. If she had more of an idea of why we were laughing, she did not let on, but at least we were laughing. It felt good, and I could tell I was smiling. Even if I could not see my face in the beaten-up window. The laughter, on my part, faded into a sigh.

My phone reminded me of its presence, and the fact that someone wanted to get ahold of me. Insistent, the vibration refused to stop for more than a few seconds. Text after text after text flooded in, I could feel them. Maybe some were imaginary sensations, but I doubted that.

I pulled the phone out of my pocket and saw the screen light up as another message came through: *Where are you?*

You missed the first go.

HELLOOOOOOOOOOOOOO?

Come on, M.

You need to report in. Now.

M. That made me laugh again, being reduced to a single, solitary letter. The sound drew another look from Charlie.

A shiver went through me, and I started thumbing out a response.

Something came up. A lie, if only by the omission that I am what came up. My lack of being, or wanting to be—whether perceived or to exist—got in the way of me getting off of the bus.

I'm not feeling like myself. Appended to the message, not firing off fast, staccato texts like I usually would. Knowing that the three-bouncing-dots I kept alive by thumbing, deleting, and adding more, drove the faceless void on the other side of the digital tether up a wall made me smile. A twist of the lips, threatening to shatter my face like hastily constructed paper mâché.

"Penny for your thoughts?" Charlie's voice drew me back to the moment and away from my phone. Her eyes pierced through me and fastened me to the seat, managing to do so through the reflection in the mirror. I locked my gaze with hers, opened my mouth to speak, and bit my tongue at the same time, somehow.

I closed my mouth again, at a loss.

"I get it. There's a lot going on, and you're feeling worn through, right? Just need a moment to pause and take a break? To wake up. I've been there, done that, got the t-shirt, and lost it all at the same time." Charlie's voice was warm in a familiar sort of way. That struck me again, that I remembered her, somehow.

"I am fine?" My voice, distant, betrayed me as it lilted up in a question. I paused, drew a deep breath, and before I could reason out why, I kept speaking. "I am not fine," I admitted, shaking my head. As if I released a pressure valve, steam poured out. "I am torn between one day and the next, do this, do that, be this, be that. I feel like I cannot breathe in my own skin, even for a moment—" I paused, and did just that. I drew a deep, shuddering, all-encompassing breath and held it.

"It's okay to say no. Just not today. You have somewhere to be. Something really important to do, right? Right." Charlie nodded with her words. "Tomorrow, though? Tomorrow, you can do whatever you want. Go wherever you want. Be whatever you want. Today, though? Look at me."

That statement drew my attention, and I found myself drowning in those green eyes.

"Do what you have to, to get through. Just…breathe, M. It's not too late."

When I let it go, I, too, let go of some of the weight sitting on my chest that I had carried for so long. I felt it slough away like a second skin, and Charlie smirked as she watched me. My gaze shifted from her to the window. Night had well and truly fallen. The streetlights, yellow and wan, cast the world in a sepia sort of tone.

"Watch out," I shouted, as if that would help. Too late, someone stepped off the curb. In the way of accidents—in the way the world itself slows down—the details became crystalline, seared into my mind. A shocked face, looking up at the bus as this lady stepped right in front of it. Their companion, a face locked between fear and anger, his mouth open, his hand outstretched. A face full of regret.

Charlie, though.

That look. That knowing look.

She called me M. *Shit.*

"It'll be okay," Charlie offered, but I had serious doubts.

The bus collided into someone with a loud thud. The sound of metal on something soft preceded a bastion of shocked silence. Raindrops fell on the windshield, the gore of them streaking downward. Someone screamed, and it might have been me. More shouts followed. The world froze, if only for a moment, as the brakes engaged. The bus skittered and came to a sudden stop.

Too late.

"Fuck." Charlie, standing from her seat. "Oh fuck. Oh shit, no." She continued to stare in shock out the door, repeating a multitude of variations of those words.

The want to be anywhere else hit me hard. Bile rose into my throat, and I turned away from the macabre display painted crimson and black across the front of the bus. A siren sounded in the distance, growing closer with every panicked breath I took. I stood, and without much more thought, ran toward the back of the bus. I slammed into the rear doors as I tried getting as far away from the—*No. Not going to think about that.* My stomach clenched as I kicked the doors open, spilled out into the growing crowd. Shouts assaulted my ears, someone tried to stop me, stood in my way.

"Sir! Stop! You can't leave, the cops are going to need a statement!"

"What happened? What was the driver thinking?"

Too many people crowding in.

Too many voices assaulting my ears.

Too many faces shoving into mine.

Too many.

Someone snapped my picture, maybe a picture of the bus. I shied away as multiple phones pointed my way, flashes firing off with miniature explosions of light. I shoved people aside to escape.

To run away from Charlie, and that look. *That look.*

She never even hit the brakes until it was too late.

I fought my way free of the crowd, throwing elbows at anyone who crowded in further, until I could part the sea of flesh. I found freedom and took off, rounding the corner, colliding with another person.

"Hey! Watch where you're going! Creep!" Her face, too close, I saw the makeup, the mascara, the wings at the corner of her eyes. The pale lip-gloss, lipstick, whatever it's called. I saw the splattering of freckles across the bridge of her nose, the deep brown of her eyes. Her hair, done in a series of buns, a mixture of purple and black. Shorter than me, but stronger as she shoved me away.

"Sorry, sorry, I just—I'm sorry."

She pushed past me, and I kept stumbling forward, away from the sirens and din behind me, the screams, the shouts, everything. I ran, slowed to a walk, and ran again, panic setting in. I zigged around another corner, and zagged across a street, focusing on just putting as much distance behind me as I could. I gathered the fabric of my pants up, so I did not trip over the long hem, struggling to tighten the belt.

Concentrating, biting my lip as pain shot through my body, I dared not stop. I hunched over, for a moment, placing my hand against the store window. Neon, flashing lights painted my skin with strobing hues. I coughed, spat something out, closed my eyes as a wave of nausea washed over me.

"Hey, uh, miss? Are you alright?" A voice, nearby. Too close.

"Yes, I'm fine." My voice, not my own, came out unfamiliar to my ears. I looked up enough to watch the concerned individual pause, as if to say something else, before they thought better of it and hurried on their way.

After a moment of breathing, I stood and caught my reflection in the store window. I fixed one of the black and purple buns on my head that had gone askew.

Part of the window, where an ad had been posted, obscured my face, but I could at least fix my hair before I turned and walked away, looking at my phone.

Something came up. Not feeling like myself. I need a few days to find myself.

I hit send, powered off my phone, throwing it into a trashcan as I passed by, and walked.

L'appel du Vide

F EAR SPIKED HARD AND deep into Remi's core. His gaze roved over the city sprawling out beneath him.

Vertigo slammed into him, blurring the world at the edges.

The city below shifted and danced, vibrating in a dizzying way. Bile rose into his throat and for a brief moment that somehow still lingered, Remi wanted to jump.

For no reason other than he could, to plummet straight to the ground.

He could picture it, the rush of the wind burning against his face. The sudden, inevitable impact of concrete, or a tree first and then the concrete, rushing up fast to meet him.

L'appel du vide, a term his therapist used, one that made a certain sort of sense.

The call of the void. The story of his life, whenever his mind wandered.

Sudden, dark, intrusive thoughts plagued him day in, day out, and most nights too. Swallowing hard against the thought that lingered long past its unwelcome appearance, Remi cleared his throat, his foot hovered over the edge, tension binding his muscles.

Darlie piped up somewhere behind him, "Slow your roll, Remi. Not yet."

Remi put his foot down literally, tried to do so figuratively as he looked away from both her, and the side of the building. "I'm not sure I want to do this, Darlie."

"I'm not sure you have a choice." She turned his face back to her. "I hate to do this, and was hoping you wouldn't make me, but you owe me. One last job. I know what you did, what no one else knows. The rain, the car accident. That you caused, dropping your bag on your first flight."

Another spike of fear lanced Remi, and he wanted nothing more than to follow his flight-response, to get away from Darlie. He pushed his glasses further up his nose subconsciously.

She left him no choice.

"It's a real simple job this time. You have a series of deliveries to make, lickety-split, that's it, Remi Q." Darlie tried to smile.

Remi nodded, his hand running through rain and sweat-slicked curls, drawing them away from his forehead, not that they stayed in place, flopping back down. "You know I hate it when you call me that, Darlie. Are you ready?"

"Almost. Anyway, what's with the hurry?" She shot him a considering look. "You got a hot date or something more important than this?" Half laughing as she came up beside him, digging through the leather messenger bag at her side, she nudged him with her elbow. Locks of red hair escaped her checkered black and white hat. Green eyes stared him down as he faced her. She searched his face, and that half smirk on her lips spoke to the fact that she might just already know the answer and enjoyed watching him squirm.

"Yes—" Remi blinked, realizing the words about to come out of his mouth, he shook his head. "I mean, no."

"Which is it?" Darlie raised an eyebrow as she looked at him. Through him, as if she could see into his darkest, most secret parts.

Remi always thought Darlie could read him like a book. Hell, most everyone could, his face expressive even when he wished otherwise. Even then, he felt heat creep into his cheeks. "That is to say, yes, I have a date. And no, it's not more important than this. I promise I'm focused on the job at hand." He tried to offer a smile, even if it ached to do so.

"I see," Darlie said, drawing out the final syllable. "Do you want to tell me about him? Might help take your mind off of overthinking this." The look on her face, though, spoke to more than just a willingness to listen. A raw hunger for information telegraphed itself in her features.

"Simon." Even saying his name, Remi couldn't help but smile as his heart fluttered. That, at least, helped drive away the last intrusive thoughts from the nooks and crannies of his mind.

"Tell me about this Simon—"

"No." He shook his head. "I mean, uh, not right now. Not yet. Maybe later? We have work to do. I'd rather not dwell on my date. I'm nervous enough as it is. If I do? I'm going to lose my nerve across the board."

"Suit yourself." Darlie's long, lithe fingers latched onto the lapels of his jacket, turning him to fully face her, pulling him away from the ledge. Away from the unsteadiness of seeing the city so far below.

Thirty floors up, Remi could see for what felt like years. The coming and going of groups of ant-like humans, of slightly larger cars, flooding through the streets. Even as Darlie turned him, his gaze lingered on the city until he'd hurt his neck if he didn't relent.

Letting go, he came face to face with those striking green eyes. Similar in color to Simon's, but with a much sharper edge in their regard. Remi's heart fluttered at Darlie's nearness, and he licked his wind-chapped lips, blinking behind his glasses.

"Hello again," he managed to say without a squeak.

"Are you ready?" she whispered, as if someone might hear them. As if the wind from so high up might steal her words away, to where someone else might overhear, might recognize what they were about, might care.

"No, but then again, I never really am." Adrenaline already coursed through his veins, thrumming in his heart, hotwiring the circuits of his brain. Part of him, fearful, dreading what was to come.

The rest of him, though? Waited with bated breath. Breath that came with difficulty, this high up.

Darlie leaned over and adjusted the harness they'd fit beneath his jacket. Her hands wandered.

At first, Remi thought she might be getting amorous to distract him, but realized that she started tugging his jacket off when the cold crept in. A shiver thrummed through his body.

"Are you sure you're going to manage this?" Concern crept into Darlie's voice as she checked, double-checked, and tightened the harness a third time. "This will be the longest flight yet. And you have to stay high, out of sight." She looked at him with concern.

"I know. I know." Remi shivered as he grinned. "I've got this." *I think.* Doubt threatened to creep in on the steep slope of anxiety, but adrenaline ensured it found no purchase.

"We really do need to get you a proper suit put together. Something warmer at least," Darlie teased, noticing how he shivered every time the wind blew. Up there, the wind stole warmth as easily as it blew with no impediment, with no other buildings standing in its way.

And here I stand, the last bastion against wind that has traveled so far, making it move out of my way, Remi thought to himself, focusing his attention on anything but Darlie's nearness, her scent intoxicating and warm, full of spice and life. Her hands, smoothing his shirt, adjusting the leather straps here, there, everywhere it seemed like, for the umpteenth time.

"Tell me the plan again." She withdrew enough to stare up at him, drawing his attention back to her.

Remi grew anxious, fighting not to shuffle from foot to foot. "Again?"

"Yes. I would like to hear it all again." Darlie stepped back further, giving him space, those green eyes, vivid and intent on him.

He fidgeted, taking a strap out of his pocket, adjusting it to secure his glasses. *Not worth losing those again.* Rolling his eyes and collecting his thoughts, he looked over the edge of the building. He checked the straps again, as if Darlie had not repeatedly done so.

Remi caught her gaze and grinned as he fastened his earbuds into place. The din of the wind and the world died under the noise-canceling feature. "Step one? Jump."

He did just that, leaping off the edge. He saw her mouth open, barely heard the scream of surprise as she leaned over to watch him fall. The music kicked on, drowning out the sudden surge of wind whistling past him.

Losing himself in the music, any lingering doubt or fear melted away with the gust of wind rushing beneath him, lifting him into the air. Gravity tried to assert itself but ultimately failed.

Remi felt that gut-lurching wrench, right then and there, that somehow, he would fail. Fall. To the ground. Leave behind little more than a smear, a mess for someone else to clean up.

He almost let go of the wind, almost let himself do just that.

But no. The tight leather bands remained so against his chest, but he still wondered if he should've checked *one more time*. They rattled but remained firm, tight against him, constricting and bearing the small devices, latent reminders of why he flew. This time, at least.

Following the thread of wind, Remi let himself simply wander through the air, letting it ruffle through his locks, pressing his glasses tighter to his face. He circled the skyscraper once, twice, and a third time, orienting himself to the layout of the city.

Darlie had drilled the aerial map into his mind, but it paled in comparison to his literal bird's eye view.

Constantly moving and daring not to stop, he plotted out his trajectory between gulps of breath and thrumming heartbeats.

After finding his bearing, Remi took off along Chestnut Street. Swooping through the air, between buildings, taking updrafts when he needed to be higher and compacting himself when he needed to be lower. No matter what, his gaze remained centered on the building a few blocks up the street.

While it was the focal point of his flightpath, he knew he had to be careful to stay away from it, to stay higher up. Darlie's warnings echoed in his mind. *Stay high, out of sight.* And so, he did, following the course of the streets, but higher in the air. Within a block, he veered to the right, down Theater Drive.

Sinking lower, to where he could almost touch the buildings as he passed over them, Remi flew. Skimming across roofs, he counted, anticipating the *BEEP.* Wincing at that loud noise piercing into his ear, he unlatched the first part of the plan; removing one of the objects firmly attached to his harness. Taking one of the metal, cylindrical objects, he twisted it like Darlie had shown him over and over. He waited, plotting the trajectory as best he could. It didn't have to be perfect, but it had to be—*now.*

Remi dropped the canister, listened to it whistle as it descended on a tangent from his path, arcing toward the building behind him. Unable to look away, lest he crash into something, the second *BEEP-BEEP* told him the device landed, awaiting deployment.

Good. So far, so good. He allowed himself a moment to breathe easily, or at least with less anxiety, as the rushing wind barely let him catch his breath.

The sudden ringing of his phone nearly caused him to drop the next device, and he panicked, wondering whether he should answer. Whether Darlie had some vital update. He couldn't risk not answering. The next near-deafening ringing cut off as Remi pushed the earbud to accept the call. Silence greeted him at first, lingering like an echo in his ears.

"Hello?" he shouted, even though he tried not to, trying to hear over the rushing wind.

"Hi." One word, one very timid voice, which had the propensity to short-circuit Remi's brain. Which it did.

Shit. "Hello there." Despite the cold burn of the wind, or maybe emboldened by it, he felt his cheeks grow warm. "Simon." Even saying that name made him smile enough that it almost hurt. "Is everything okay?"

"Yes, yes, I just wanted to call—where are you, Remi? It sounds like you're in a wind tunnel." Simon's words lilted upward, making his words more like a question.

"I'm taking care of one last thing for work." He winced after making sure his path was clear.

"Work." Simon's distaste flooded the line. He spoke up, as if he could overcome the sound of the wind as well. "Do you have a moment to get somewhere more, well, quiet?"

Remi flinched. "Not just yet, no."

"Remi. Tonight is supposed to be really special. Just us. You *promised*. After all these dates we've missed, or you've been late to, leaving me in a lurch with wasted tickets, or even my family, I really wanted tonight to work."

"Hold that thought. Hold on a moment." He tried not to panic even as adrenaline spiked through his system. More than he already had coursing through him. Another *BEEP* made him recoil. He dropped the next cylinder, relying on his muscle memory.

"Remi?" Simon spoke a little louder.

"Shit. I know. I'm sorry, it's just—"

BEEP-BEEP.

"I just wanted to hear your voice. Calm me down before tonight." Simon giggled, and Remi felt the same sound building in his own nerves. "I wanted to make sure you were running on schedule. That we didn't have to cancel." *Again.* Simon hardly had to say it.

Remi knew it lurked, unspoken, between them. "I know. I was thinking about calling you too." He tried to catch his breath. "I'm so very glad to hear that. I mean, for the same reason." He tried not to shout, the natural urge when facing gale-force winds. He didn't dare land, not yet. "I'm going to be there. I promise. I'm already almost done with work. It won't interfere tonight. I promise. The reservations are made, I have a nice suit picked out. Six o'clock, sharp."

"You picked one out for me, too." Simon sounded half upset, and half amused.

"Well, I, uh, ah. I saw it, and thought of you, and—"

"Shh. Don't fret. It's okay, just a surprise is all. A nice one," Simon added, after a pause, laughter still painting his words with warmth.

Remi sighed. "Listen, I have to finish up this work."

"Always working." A pause. "And you hate to say goodbye. I get it." Simon laughed again. "I'll save you that. I'm looking forward to tonight, Remi. Don't forget about me." Another pause, filled with that silently spoken *again*. "I'll see you later, gator. Chomp chomp."

Before Remi could say anything, the line went dead, replaced as his music picked up again. Another *BEEP* sounded. Thoughts of Simon raced through his head, distracting him enough that he almost missed the cue to unhook the next device, to prepare himself. He swallowed hard, knowing if he did, he'd have to re-orient and figure out a new pattern, a new trajectory, all on the fly.

Damn it. Pay attention, Remi Q.

Shaking his head, Remi fumbled with the next cylinder and nearly dropped it too early. Maybe too late. His mind blanked on where he was in the process, with Simon's face overwriting the details of the job. He looked down—against his better judgment, his heart in his throat—to watch the device on its tangent. Certain that the arc of its descent might carry it right over the edge. That he missed this target.

He sighed in relief as it thunked and rolled on the roof.

BEEP-BEEP.

Close call.

Fighting to control his breathing, and to clear his mind much the way his therapist had taught him, Remi focused. Another drop, another set of loud beeps, and he twisted, turning himself in midair as he redirected his flightpath. Enjoying the struggle of wrestling with, and against, the wind, he sighed deeply. Circling back, creating a large circle around a central point, he noticed the building in the center.

A tall, spired building, covered on all sides with unassuming windows. As he kept it to his left well below him, he watched the workers droning away inside. He almost felt bad for them, so high in the air and unable to feel it, to ride it, to dance within it like he could.

Shoving them out of his mind, and picking his altitude back up, he listened for the next series of beeps, followed by the corresponding double beeps. Four more devices placed on four more rooftops, and as usual, his time to fly came to an end.

By the time he circled back where he started, Remi couldn't spot Darlie anywhere. Panic settled like a web over his heart, grasping and entangling him. Despite the temptation to kick higher into the air and risk another lap, he decided to land. *Simon.*

Slowing himself as he landed, his shoes skidded across the rough roof. It took all he had to stop, grounding himself once more to the terrestrial plane. As if the wind itself didn't want to let him go, he had to fight against the urge to take off again, to release the ground.

To never touch it again.

Remi grimaced, shuddering as gravity settled around him, a smothering, heavy blanket. It hurt to breathe, his chest tight, as if something sat on him.

"Fuck." He barely managed to whisper around a slowly closing throat. He fell to his knees, the weight of the world itself resting on his shoulders as gravity reasserted itself with a vengeance. He felt like Sisyphus after an eon of battling that rock up the hill, defeated, letting it crush him.

Inhaling eased a little, enough that it drove away the fugue settling over his mind. Pins and needles assaulted his extremities; he realized he'd fallen onto his stomach, staring at a closeup of the roof's rough, tarred surface.

Numb fingers reached for his Epi-pen first, before remembering Darlie had it. Instead, he reached for his phone, drawing it out of his pocket. Hardly able to lift his arm or his head, Remi fumbled to stand it sideways against the roof ledge to at least read the time; 5:45 PM.

"Shit." Fighting against gravity's revenge for daring to be free of it, Remi struggled to breathe, to focus, as if the air itself were pressing down on him, like he was little more than a spider beneath a boot. Thumbing his earbud, he activated the chirrup of the digital assistant. "Call..." His voice trailed off, paralyzed by the fact he had to make a choice. Darlie, or Simon? Simon, or Darlie? One would never forgive him. The other could only save him. The phone beeped at him, almost quiet compared to the device's sounds.

Breathless, hoping against all reason, barely able to hear his own voice, he hoped the mystical, magical phone-lady would hear his demand. "Call Simon." Black spots filled the corners of his vision, but Remi screwed his eyes shut against them, as if that might remotely help.

The harsh noise of the ringing filled his ears, tears ran as he willed his body to listen. *Not yet. Please. Not yet.* As if that had ever worked. Remi tried to throw off the shackles of gravity, even enough to sit up, to draw a full breath, enough to stay awake. *Just a few more moments. Please.*

The call connected to silence.

"I'm sorry," he whispered with all the breath he had left, his vision dimming further.

"You promised me. Don't do this to me, not again. Remi."

Simon's pained, broken utterance of his name was the last thing he heard before falling into the dark rabbit hole of unconsciousness.

"Wake up, Remi," Darlie said between sobs, though her voice sounded so far away.

His back arched as if he might bend enough to completely snap in two. His mouth opened in a silent scream; he felt his chapped lips split first before agony flooded his body. It radiated from the center of his chest, his heart speeding a mile-a-minute, and the Epi-pen needle sticking out of him. Or rather, into him.

"Fuck!"

Remi screamed, and screamed, the adrenaline coursing through him, pain searing every fiber of his being.

Bit by bit, light crept back into the world, as did his ability to focus. Amorphous blobs of colors coalesced into a pair of green eyes, wide and worried, staring at him.

"Remi, Kentucky Fucking Chicken. I'm so sorry, I had to go to the bathroom, and then the door back out here got stuck. Oh fuck, oh fuck, ah shit. I am *so* sorry. Fuck. Are you okay? Tell me you're okay. Please. You have to be okay." She shook him, as if that'd help her pleading to him, that both could fix all that had gone horribly, unbelievably wrong.

Remi bit his tongue for another—this time, *controlled*—source of pain. It drowned out some of the rest, even as Darlie shook him like a rattle again. It also kept him from screaming right into her face, unleashing the anguish that sat dead in the middle of his chest.

"What...time...is...it?" he barely managed to speak through chattering teeth, cold ravaging his body. Not that he needed to ask that question.

Simon's voice repeated his name on the wind as the fading sun in the distance, dipping almost completely below the horizon, told him all he needed to know.

It's too late.

Pushing away from Darlie, he sat up, wobbling all the way. He nearly collapsed, but sheer determination kept him from doing so. He searched for his phone.

Fingers slipped against it, not quite willing to listen to his commands, but when he finally managed to flip it over, a cracked screen glared at him. He sighed and tried the phone anyways, despite the slight bend in the body. The screen came to life, if only for a moment, before it puttered out and went dark.

"No, no, nonononononono." Remi shook his head and tried to stand up, stumbling.

Darlie shot to her feet first and caught him as he nearly tumbled, too close to the edge for his liking as his heart slammed downward, as if it meant to evacuate his body completely.

"It'll be okay, Remi Q," she said, squeezing him, trying to offer comfort.

She might've been about to say something else before he blinked owlishly at her, shaking his head, gritting his teeth. "I *promised* Simon I would be there tonight. On time, for once." He ran a hand through his hair, before he started tearing at the buckles and straps of the harness, letting it slither off of him. "And that's gone, now."

"Remi, I—"

"Weren't there for me. Nearly *let me die.* And worse, this isn't the first time you've fucked up my life." He shook his head, looking toward the edge of the building. Toward the updrafts of air calling his name.

"I'm sorry, I—"

"You have what you needed, Darlie. Lose my number. No more, no more of this. My debt is clear, you aren't going to hold the accident over me. Not anymore. I am *done.*" When she opened her mouth to speak again, he snarled, *"Done!* I've wanted out for some time, and this is it." He convulsed, the adrenaline driving a pervasive chill through him. Stomping his feet, trying to spread warmth through himself, stop the shaking before it started. "In fact, I'll just get a new phone number altogether. Damn it, Darlie." He held a hand up, forestalling anything else she might have said when she opened her mouth again.

A few moments of silence passed, Darlie opening, closing, and opening her mouth again only to swallow hard, and nod. "I'll see that your payment is deposited. That's it. I'll let you be, nice and quiet like. And I'll tell the others that you're off-limits." She looked anywhere but at him, which served him just fine.

Turning away from her, limping, struggling against the heavy weight of every step, he hurried toward the door.

Maybe Simon is still waiting.

Remi knew better, though.

The Unbearable Weight of Time

*T*HE WEIGHT OF THIRTY *seconds can become unbearable, and time itself can cease to hold meaning in moments of extreme duress. Any slice of time, sufficiently crammed full of emotion, is prone to speeding up or slowing down, and not always in the way one might prefer. And even the smallest incongruence can take one out of the stream. Time can mean everything, and nothing, and sometimes both at once.*

Once.

Sabrina stared at that word on the screen, the cursor flashing after the period. Her mind emptied itself of any remaining thoughts before making her fingers *click clack* across the keyboard. Transforming the motions of her fingers into transcribing erratic thoughts.

Silence followed as her hands came to rest against her desk, her eyes locked on the cursor, as if that might will the words to flow with no one to press the keys. The lights cascaded within her keyboard still, a myriad of rainbow colors teasing her. Mocking her.

"Come on, Sabrina. Think. Write the words. You can do it!" Urging herself even as she tried to get her brain working, Sabrina felt the familiar surface of the wall as she ran right into it. That which separated her from the words she yearned to find, to put voice to the sensations crawling around in her brain, eager to be free, born into stories loosed into the world. She had yet to figure out how to break past it. Or which combination to use to unlock it. Whether to plant seed words, from which the next idea might grow, watered with the right playlist, or a glance out the window to catch natural inspiration.

Nothing struck the mood. Every *tick* and *tock* of the clock reminded her, even if she managed to not pay it attention, that time moved inexorably forward. It slowly ran out. Or quickly, because sometimes ten seconds felt like thirty minutes, and hours passed like anxious breaths.

In the blink of an eye, one heartbeat to the next, time slipped away through her fingers.

Frustrated and knowing no words were forthcoming, Sabrina hit save, closed the document, and stared at the clutter of icons on her desktop obscuring the current wallpaper, a mock motivational image that made her laugh every time she glanced at it. *Almost* every time she glanced at it.

Sabrina couldn't bring herself to laugh. Instead, she locked the computer and powered off the monitors. Before she could catch her own reflection in the dark screen, she pushed away from the desk and stood before tucking her chair back in. Yanking on the overhead cord, she turned the ceiling lights off. She left the fan running. She hated coming back home to an office full of stale air.

"Hold your horses," Sabrina muttered. Her phone dinged at her from its cradle in her breast pocket. Fishing it out, she stared at the notification on the screen. Ignoring the content of the text, she focused on the sender.

An unknown number.

She sighed, heavy and hard. Any hopes she had of taking a quick walk was dashed against the mountain of work expectations. Thumb against the screen, she unlocked the phone and flicked the message open as it dinged a few more times.

Hey. We need to meet up.

It's almost go-time and things are progressing to plan. Almost.

We need to meet.

Okay, I hate to pull this card. You need to check in. Usual place, my treat. -Tarly

From a new number, a new burner. That confirmed Tarly behind the messages.

"I'll be there." Sabrina bit her lip, mumbling out the words, letting her phone dictate the text for her. Never trusted her fingers much to move fast enough for her brain, even when it came to short messages. "I've been looking at the projections, and you're right. Things are *almost* to plan. But we're going to have to adjust. Maybe. I think."

She spoke more to the phone than into it, waiting for its dictation to catch up to her train of thought while wandering through her apartment, until she stopped at the expansive windows that overlooked the city. Here, she could—and often did—stand, watching the city move. A beating heart full of people in its geometric veins, who flit in front of the sunset-lit windows, like motes blotting out the sun. Gazing down at the street choking on innumerable moving cars, she could almost feel the world thrum under so many footsteps, a raging rapids of human movement.

Staring out, Sabrina could almost imagine herself as timeless, frozen, outside of the world, looking in.

She hit send on the phone. Pocketed it again, and tore herself away from the window. Grabbing her father's old army jacket, she drew it on as she tied her hair up into a messy bun. Tried to remember the last time she booked a haircut.

Before her last therapy session. "Yikes."

She grabbed her keys from where they hung, locking the door behind her. Before she knew it, she found herself at the street level, waiting for the perfect moment to leave the stoop to her building and enter the unceasing flow of people. There, in between two almost-synchronized groups, Sabrina found a place to step into the tide.

A few blocks up, she waited for the little flashing man to clear the street for her. This belief persisted since childhood, that the tiny glowing figure of light made traffic stop with some arcane, eldritch power. She held her position on the curb, counting out three seconds as she leaned back. An oncoming car sped through the intersection, through the red light, barely paying a lick of attention. Sabrina sighed, glad to not be pâté on the pavement.

As she crossed the street, her eyes glued themselves to the coffee shop two blocks up the street.

Well, to the sign at least, which hung high enough from the building that she could see it over the crowd. The sign, *Java Nice Day*, grew steadily, slower than she liked, until it was right above her. She stared into and through her reflection in the glass door, trying to see if Tarly had arrived yet.

"Guess I'm early," Sabrina muttered to herself as she opened the door with a hearty yank, nearly tripping over the threshold as she stepped in.

Immediately, the aroma and warmth of coffee enveloped her, suffusing her with a heady feeling. Already, her heart raced as she stepped into the short line at the counter, glancing over both the menu behind the baristas, who buzzed around like bees, and the monitor displaying Web and App orders.

Tarly. That familiar name, at the top of the online order list, drew her attention like a beacon.

Fishing her wallet out of her pocket, Sabrina stepped forward once the customers ahead of her stepped to the side. Her attention flitted to the window and back to her wallet, causing her to bump into the counter, dropping a small handful of coins. She looked up and came face to face with a barista. One with an entirely too perky attitude, her blonde ponytail practically dancing with her energy.

"Hi! Welcome to Java Nice Day. Would you like to try any of our specials of the week? Mocha Cookie Crumble Cold Brew? Black Lilac Caramel Chai? Or how about the Hazelnut Mocha Latte?"

"Hi"—Sabrina, surprised at the throatiness of her own words, glanced down at the barista's nametag before bringing her gaze back up slowly—"Therese."

She felt like she moved through molasses, a sweet, syrupy haze clouding her vision of the barista. Either Sabrina herself was dragging ass that bad, or the barista had been ingesting pure caffeine. Maybe the coffee dust permeating the air from the near-constant grinding infused her very blood. If Sabrina moved slowly, the girl across the counter moved at light speed. Whatever it was, Sabrina could not tear her eyes away from Therese, which let her notice the way the barista eyed her back.

"Listen. Uh—" Sabrina paused, lifting a hand to scratch the back of her neck. "I'm paying for Tarly's order for her. I'm meeting her here, and it seems I'm early." When the barista seemed ready to argue, or ask a question, Sabrina cut her off, recounting the order.

"Oh, oh, okay! That'll be—"

"Here." Sabrina offered the money over, plus some for a tip. No point in pissing Tarly off.

"—$32.50." Therese looked down at the money already in her hand. "Oh?" The confusion clear on her face spoke to her brain short-circuiting at the amount of money, or maybe the way their fingers barely grazed, a static shock leaping between them.

"It's all there, and more to boot. For you. A tip." Sabrina offered a slight, coy smile, leaning in a little. "Because I know this is going to be the greatest coffee I've had yet today. Maybe this week. I mean, what, made by my own personal coffee fairy princess?" Sabrina winked as Therese blushed.

Therese timidly retrieved the order and placed it on a tray for Sabrina. The way she shot looks at her, the barista still had a healthy blush on her soft cheeks. Sabrina felt her own face grow warm.

Therese opened her mouth, seemed about to say something.

"I haven't seen you here before, either, but I can see myself coming much more often," Sabrina offered, smirking. "Maybe we will see each other again." She even threw in a slick wink—*where did that come from?*—as she took the tray and left Therese standing there with her mouth hanging open, her face growing a few shades redder.

With the coffee cups on the tray tantalizingly close to her mouth, and entirely too far away, Sabrina breathed as deep as she could instead, inhaling the aroma as she nimbly sidestepped the kitchen door, thrust open as the busser backed out of it, rolling a mop and bucket.

There, a table in the corner, facing as many of the doors as possible. And with nothing but solid walls behind it. Where she almost half expected to see Tarly sitting anyway, but no. *Not yet. I'm early, for once.* Sabrina set down the tray and sat in Tarly's seat. She'd only keep it warm, because sitting there herself would bother Tarly.

She leaned back in the chair, stretching her arms over her head before reaching for one of the cups on the tray. She sipped at her coffee, letting her eyes wander over the café. And its occupants.

Brows furrowing together, Sabrina observed the customers, wondering where they all came from, where they would inevitably go, leaving minimal traces of their presences that the next patron would overwrite with their own. Echoes, ripples of lives played out in real time. Patterns in coffee stains and sugar granules spread over a table. One in particular that, if she stared at it long enough, she felt might help her figure out how all the puzzle pieces fit.

After watching the people come and go for a while, Sabrina stood and moved to the other side of the small table, taking her rightful seat. With the café behind her, she contented herself with looking out the window, its light spreading over the table between her and the glass.

Across the street, someone ducking and weaving along the sidewalk—as if they feared someone might be following them—caught her attention.

Sabrina tracked their movements twisting in her seat as they disappeared around the corner, reappearing in the next window over, striding for the door. They yanked it open and entered, a large hat pulled low on their head, large sunglasses obscuring a good part of their face.

She smirked at the conspicuously inconspicuous person as they slid into the seat across from her.

"I see we're actually early today, Sabrina." Tarly took off her sunglasses as she spoke, a tired set of green eyes staring at her.

"Well, I do live closer. And I needed coffee." She took another sip, eying her.

Tarly shot her a knowing look. "Words still aren't flowing, huh?"

"Not as much as I might like, but I did manage *some* writing today." Sabrina couldn't keep the Cheshire grin off of her face as she spotted Therese in the distance, their eyes meeting for the briefest exchange. Sabrina bit her lip, looking back at Tarly. "What's with the cloak and daggers?"

"Oh, that." Tarly's nose wrinkled up as she sighed. "This is close to where Felix's currently holed up, and on the off chance he's decided to crawl out of his cave, well..." she trailed off, grimacing.

"Right, right. That makes sense." Sabrina exchanged her empty coffee for the other one on the tray as Tarly dug into her own part of the order. "I am honestly a little surprised we're meeting already."

"Well, with the way this is panning out, M has gone to ground. Felix is, well. You know that story already." Tarly shrugged, waving her hand dismissively in the air. "I have to start hammering down the unknowns, and well..."

"You aren't going to offend me." Sabrina chuckled. "Out with it."

"You're hard to pin down at the best of times. With everything else going on, I figured a check-in was in order. Gives us a chance to at least chitchat, too." She tried to smile, tried to hide thoughts lurking behind the darting of her eyes. How very tired she looked, how very worn-through.

Sabrina had felt the same lately. That the day-in and day-out became the same thing, over and over and over. "This close, we have to ensure the pieces are in order. All of them. I get it. And Felix isn't the only one who lost someone, is he?" She poked, more out of curiosity, morbid as it might've been, than anything else.

Tarly withdrew behind a stony façade, her eyes guarded. "I guess."

"Listen, Marlie will be missed. That's all I mean. Are you okay?"

"Something like that," Tarly groused, albeit good-naturedly. "It's not that bad. Felix, though. That's bad. Could be, at least. I don't know." She sighed and shook her head, looking anywhere but at her.

"Riiiight." Sabrina arched an eyebrow, sipping at her coffee. "I think you're still in the shock phase of losing someone, too. Might need to slow down and breathe."

"Sure, that's it," Tarly half growled, shaking her head as she swiveled on her. "Keep pushing and see where that gets you."

"No one's pushing, Tarl. No one, not me. Not like that. Obviously I get it. Whatever you're dealing with, know that I care. That's it. That's all. Much the same as Felix does. We'll all miss Marlie." Sabrina spat the last part out, perhaps a little more vehemently than intended, and that earned her another glare. A hard one. She set the cup down and raised her hands placatingly. "Listen. Fine. I'll shut up about it. Okay? Now, as for the rest of everything?"

Tarly set her own cup down, her face looking as tired as Sabrina felt. "I was hoping you could shed some more light on the coming days. Something's off. I was hoping it'd be all nice and quiet like."

"Not as much light as you might hope. It's too soon. I'm no good this early. I can't get a good glance at much of anything past today." She shook her head. And yet, could not deny that a part of her wanted to try. That look Tarly gave her, the one of a certain level of disappointment, drove a spike into her stomach. A want, a *need* to help, however she could. No matter the cost.

"I see." Tarly pursed her lips and stood. "I'll continue to monitor the plan and situation. Make sure that *you* are ready when the time comes. We will see to the rest, and that all the players are in place."

"Even Felix? Listen, I think we're going to need him."

Tarly sighed. "Is that your...professional...opinion?" The pause there, as she looked around the café, concerned Sabrina.

Licking her lips, Sabrina shook her head a little. "No, but you can call it a gut feeling. Something's not *right*. I haven't been able to put my finger on what. Or find the thread out of whack. But, well, whatever. Maybe I had too much Taco Bell."

"Haha, that's oh-so-very funny." Despite the grouchy tone, Tarly still cracked a smile. "I'll be in touch again soon. Real soon. Take care of yourself, Sab." With that, Tarly turned and, drawing her coat around her, ducked out the door, out onto the street, her departure as furtively enacted as her arrival.

Sabrina sighed and picked at the food Tarly hadn't bothered with, and finished off her second liquid heart attack.

After some time, she let her gaze drop to the table, back to the remnants of those who came before. Rings of coffee, a map to the past. Sugar granules strewn about, each one telling a different story, if only she knew how to listen. Sabrina let her mind wander through the mess on the table as if she would, or even could, decode it given enough time.

Instead of downing the sad dregs of her drink, Sabrina tipped it out onto the table, letting the darker grounds mix with the splattering coffee that leaked out. Her fingers danced across the surface of the table, connecting stains, making of them her own map, her own meaning.

Before Sabrina knew it, she no longer sat alone. Lifting her gaze, she came near face-to-face with Therese. Stared straight into those honey-colored eyes, with the slight ring of green gilding her irises. Sabrina's heart lurched, and not just for the excessive amounts of caffeine imbibed in a relatively short time. She tried to say something, stammering and stumbling in her attempt, and might have even blown an accidental raspberry.

"Hi. Wake up, sleepyhead." Therese sat, nervous energy all too evident as she fidgeted with her own drink, alternating between holding it, setting it down, moving it away from Sabrina's work on the table, and picking it back up again.

"Hi. Hello. How do you do?" Sabrina answered rapid fire, blinking out of wherever her mind wandered off to. An entire future played out in front of her, a million different possibilities, opportunities. Half tempted to let herself follow some of the livelier ones, which lead to—no—Sabrina stopped herself, a flush creeping into her cheeks. "Hi, Therese. Again."

"I just... I thought you might want to know—"

"—That that much coffee isn't good for my heart," Sabrina finished, taking the words right out of her mouth.

"Yes, that." Therese's mouth crinkled into a smile, her hands smoothing out an apron she no longer wore. "But not just that."

Sabrina leaned in a little closer. "You also wanted to say there's much more that's good for my heart, didn't you?"

Therese looked taken aback, a shake of her head to deny the words as her own face blossomed with color. "No, no—" She shook her head more vehemently.

"No? Are you *sure?*" Sabrina closed her eyes for a moment, her hand spread out against the cold surface of the table. She could feel every grain of sugar, every sticky splotch of coffee not yet dried, or long since, from the moment they spilled to now to later, when someone would invariably wipe the tables down.

"Okay, maybe I did." Therese smiled shyly. "Mind if I join you?"

"Maybe we should move to a different table." Sabrina gulped, blinking as she looked at Therese. Really looked at her, sitting across the table. Opening her mouth to point out to the barista that she already *had* joined her, Sabrina snapped it closed again as she realized it wouldn't be conducive to conversation. One of those thoughts she hardly needed to say aloud. She found herself at a loss for words. Breathing deep, Sabrina closed her eyes, her brows furrowing as she thought. Caught in between one moment and the next, she tried to find the right thing to say. Looked at all the options available to her, like one of those role-playing games she used to love but could hardly find the time to devote to anymore.

Therese's eyes crinkled up in a smile. "What, so you can dirty another table too? This one has just the right amount of light to it. And I don't want to make more work for my coworkers."

"I guess, but only if you don't actually mind my art here." Usually, her brain locked up inside of her skull, but today, Sabrina knew the right thing to say.

Words that made Therese laugh. A sound, golden in its glow, warmed by the sun streaming through the window. Her hair floated almost like an illuminated halo in that light when the laugh became so much, she shook her head.

Sabrina lost herself in the moment, prone to doing so around a pretty face. She lost track of time talking to Therese, as she often did, seeking more of those precious laughs, filing them away, storing them for later.

"I feel like I've known you for, well, forever." Therese sighed; the sound still tinged with her laugh as she wiped tears away from her eyes.

"What can I say? I've just got one of those faces." Sabrina half grinned, before her stomach dropped out. A sharp twinging chill ran through her, from her head to her toes and back again. Sweat broke out on her brow and her nape, trickling down her back. Her hackles rose, her stomach lurched. And not from the caffeine.

"What? That doesn't even make sense." And yet, Therese laughed again. A sound that warmed the cockles of Sabrina's heart, washing over that sudden tremor of fear. The café ceased to exist but for the two of them.

Sabrina opened her mouth to say something. Anything. Nothing came, and her mind stopped. She feared her heart did as well.

Shadows out of the corner of her eye caught her attention.

Three of them, to be precise.

Two men bringing up the rear behind a woman who strode past the windows with definite purpose. Each held a bundled ball of fabric in one hand, as their other hands tucked into ridiculously bulky trench coats.

Everything slowed down, everything sped up.

Sabrina fought to breathe, felt like the world sat on her chest, refusing to let her do so. "Shit. There's never enough time."

"Are you okay?" Therese leaned forward, reaching for her. "What's wrong, Sabrina?"

The fear in Therese's voice, in her own name, gave her pause. She tore her gaze away from the three people huddling just outside the door of the café. Closing her eyes, she drew a deep breath, inhaling as much as she could and then pulled in just a little more, until she felt like a balloon about to burst.

She let out the breath and sighed.

Against her better judgment, against everything she knew, Sabrina *looked forward*.

She saw straight through to tomorrow. To many tomorrows, too many tomorrows, dependent on every moment moving forward. A dizzying display of potential, of possibilities, and even yesterday, she could see the straight path that led like an arrow through the air to the very moment of *now*. A single point in time, which she revolved around herself. The here, the moment she lived in, grasped in her hand, and used it as a focal lens to look forward.

Seeing where she sat and did nothing, to where she'd stand up and walk away. Leave Therese right there, no explanation given.

To where she'd sit and continue to flirt.

To where they'd spend hours talking, until the café closed, and they remained. In control of all the music, they shared their favorite songs on the stereo system, each one bringing them closer. Until they lost track of the music and made their own.

Sabrina also saw the other possibilities. The one where she said something wrong, putting her foot in her mouth. Or Therese's coworker called in sick, forcing her back to work for a double shift. Any number of reasons that might drag them apart, any number of unforeseen paths away from one another.

For the briefest of moments, she lived through all of them, like a rock skipping across adjacent streams, until one pricked her, like a thorn. The time that wrapped around her right then, right there, cementing her in a fixed point that had nothing to do with her. All of the other possibilities faded away, leaving exactly one thread to watch, to pluck at, to rally against as it wrapped around her like a noose.

And yet here she sat. Helpless, a feeling alien to her.

Wrong time. Wrong place. Wrong *everything*.

The three newcomers changed *everything*.

Sabrina growled. "Therese. I need you to stay right here. Okay? For me, please." She looked at her, reached out, thought better of it, and took the half-drunk coffee that Tarly left behind. She swirled it in her hand, gauging how much was left.

"What's wrong? What'd I do?" Therese looked crestfallen. "Stay, please."

Sabrina grimaced. "Nothing. Not a damn thing. You did absolutely, positively nothing wrong. It's nothing. I swear. Wait right here. Right here, do you hear me? Do not move. Please. I'll be right back as soon as I can. Please, just...stay put." For a moment, the briefest of moments, she wished she had Felix there. Or his powers. Even Jasper might be of use, to get Therese out of there.

But no.

It's just me.

Therese stood, backing away from the table. "Sabrina, you're scaring me."

She sighed and held her hands out. "Please, please just listen. We're almost out of time. Sit back down. I promise I'll explain everything as soon as I can. Please." She watched Therese scan the dining area. Whether about to shout for help, to bolt, or cry, Sabrina could see all three in her eyes.

But instead, she sat back down.

Sabrina could have laughed until she cried.

Or cried until she threw up.

"Okay." Therese looked both scared and confused but remained in her seat. Watching Sabrina with a heavy, fretful look.

Good, she thought as she grabbed the half-empty coffee cup and stalked away from the table. "I'll be right back," she called over her shoulder. Looking out the doors, watching the three block the entrance, their eyes glancing up and down the street, back inside.

Surveilling the place. Casing the joint. *I know that look.*

"Fuck." Sabrina stopped next to one of the tables and closed her eyes. Chewing on her bottom lip, trying to untangle the chaos inside her mind.

She nodded to herself.

Sabrina yanked the lid from Tarly's coffee, dropping it unceremoniously on the table as she poured a decent amount out. Right on the ground. An ache built in her chest, but she shoved it down, away. Took a drink of it, even if it wasn't hers, and was down to the decidedly-less-sugary-than-she-preferred dregs at the bottom from where it had not dissolved.

It tasted like ashes against her tongue.

Every second counts. Sabrina repeated the mantra over and over and over again in her head. Despite the want to turn around, to run, she kept moving forward.

Ever forward.

Sabrina paused next to another table and cocked her head. She closed her eyes, grimacing before moving one of the chairs slightly out, cockeyed to the orientation of the table. Just enough.

It must be enough.

Cursing to herself, she spotted Therese starting to stand again, worry on her face, fear screaming from within her amber gaze. Sabrina motioned to her, mouthing the words, *Please, sit.* Pleaded with her eyes.

Therese sat back down, skepticism and a look of, *What the heck are you up to?*

Sabrina turned, setting the empty cup down. She took a moment to study the table itself before taking a nearby chair and scooting it into position. The customers at the table shot her looks.

The clock ticked.

She swore again beneath her breath.

"There." She stood closer to the counter and turned to face it, catching a barista's attention.

The door to the café opened, the little bell jingling merrily. Jarringly.

"It's go time," she whispered to herself.

She didn't have to wait long before chaos exploded. She saw it written on the barista's face; their cordial expression transmogrified into a look of absolute horror.

Sabrina smelled nervous sweat. Beneath that, more. An oily, sulfur-like smell that threatened to make her sneeze. She wanted to look over her shoulder, to confirm what she already knew, but did not.

Dared not.

"Everybody down! This is a robbery!" A male voice, harsh and loud, sounded over the onslaught of people shifting, moving, and the cacophony of screams and pained cries, the thud of the butt of a gun against flesh. "I said get down!"

Another male voice, different from the first, more nasal. "No one's a hero here, right? Got it? Even if anyone is, I'll start shooting as soon as you try a damn thing. No heroics!"

The café felt that much smaller, tighter, a sarcophagus to struggle within, threatening to swallow Sabrina. People cried. Whimpered. Whipped their phones out just before the third robber confiscated them. Slighter in stature than the others.

Sabrina stood still. Very still, as much as she wanted to run.

Every moment mattered, every moment counted, and she didn't dare let herself look toward Therese.

Sabrina fought to keep her focus in check, her breathing steady, her heart in her chest when it'd rather climb into her throat.

In between one heartbeat—rapid, frantic—and the next, one of the masked idiots must have thwacked another customer. The audible crack followed by the pained cry split the air. Every ticking second on the clock behind the counter, an epic, echoing bell tolling. One of the men, the larger one, caught Sabrina's close attention. She waited for the right moment.

"One," she whispered.

Everything clicked into place.

A scuffle broke out as the large robber reached over the table for a patron's purse. She fought him. He stumbled, his foot caught on the chair just out of place. The lady took her purse and scurried into a corner.

The diversion gave Sabrina a chance to move unnoticed.

She yanked a chair into the air and slammed it into the masked man's face. The chair shattered. She kept her fingers wrapped around the leg. It broke off in her grasp as she rounded on the second attacker.

"You stupid bitch! I'm going to—"

A startled yelp.

The nasally robber charged her, bringing his gun to bear. Aiming right for her.

Pity his foot hit the spilled coffee, sending him sliding into the chair leg Sabrina swung.

For the fences, as her father would've said.

"Two down." The bulky part of the leg met the meaty part of the man's chin, snapping his head backward. He spun backwards, head-over-heels, landing hard on his back. *If only Benny Hill were playing.*

The gun spiraled through the air. She caught the still-warm, sweat-slicked handle—*ick*—at its apex.

She spun.

Time froze again, the air a thick molasses around her. She couldn't turn fast enough. Air became sandpaper, harsh, resisting her need to move, to whirl fast enough around. Her heart plummeted from her throat.

"I'm too late." Sabrina's words were distant, twisted, to her own ears as she faced the third robber.

The last robber, who held her gun level, who aimed with her heart, had fury etched in her eyes as she screamed. "I said no heroes!"

"Three...down?"

Sabrina gulped. She could almost feel it as the robber squeezed the trigger.

Sound rushed out from the barrel before the explosion caught up and thrust the bullet forward.

Sweat dripped down Sabrina's brow as she stepped forward, her heart dead in her chest, holding her breath. Every ounce of concentration held onto the clock behind the café counter, the multitude of cell phones nearby, and further.

She swung the bloodied chair leg, tracking the bullet's trajectory and swatted it out of the air, upward, where it lodged into a thick wooden beam.

The robber's eyes widened behind her ski mask. Her fingers worked the trigger, pull, release. Pull, release. Pull, release. Rinse, repeat.

Sabrina grimaced, blood trickling from her nose, warm, coppery, salty against her lips, mixing with tears she only then realized spilled. A pigment mixed as she opened her own mouth to scream, enraged, painting her face for war. A war she fought to change.

A bullet grazed her cheekbone. She recoiled in pain. She kept her momentum, but her concentration slipped.

Sabrina screamed again. Louder. Fury building in her heart, leaping into her stomach, pouring out of her throat, into her mouth, reverberating in the air gone still.

"Three. Fuck."

She fired her borrowed gun. The robber fired her own. A deafening cacophony filled the café. Her bullet flew, hurtling, slamming through muscle, ribcage, heart.

Time worked against her, slipping through her fingers, as she tried to deflect this last bullet. Tried to alter the rail that it rode, immutable. A fixed point in time.

One that broke her heart.

Sabrina couldn't move fast enough. It flew. Past her.

She turned with it.

Therese screamed.

Blood blossomed.

Sabrina howled, redoubled her effort, grasping time again. Not to slow it, or even hold it still, but to twist it to her very will. The sharp edges of time *hurt*, but she twisted the threads of everything backward, winding it all up into a spool, screaming all the while. Sabrina closed her eyes, the tears she never felt reversing course, back into her eyes.

The world shifted.

Twisted.

Turning backward. Ever backward.

"Hi. Wake up, sleepyhead." Therese sat, nervous energy all too evident.

Not far enough.

Sabrina felt the unbearable weight of time, and pressed further, farther. She opened her eyes, and stared at the blank page, her fingers resting on the keys.

Breathing deep, she let the words flow.

Front Row Seat

On the other side of the peephole peered an eye entirely too close, making it hard for Phoebe to see. She waited for another knock to thud against the door, or for whoever it was to call out. Maybe they had already? She reached for the noise-canceling headphones and paused the classical music flooding in. Silence swept into the absence of sound.

Phoebe waited, her heart climbing into her throat as she looked at the wall separating her from the neighbor's apartment. Thankfully, she only shared one wall with anyone, what with the way her apartment sat crammed into a corner. This lessened the chance the lives of others would bleed into hers, which, in turn, meant she'd be less likely to want to listen.

A movement at the door drew her attention. Had they seen her shadow? Were they waiting for her to move away from the door? Unsure of what to do or say, Phoebe remained still. Silent. Biting her lip, her hand hovered over the lock to the door. Debated unlocking it before she checked to ensure it was fully engaged.

Another series of loud knocks beat her to it.

Phoebe nearly jumped out of her skin, skittering a few steps away from the door, clutching her sweater-coat that much closer. Her mind raced, trying to remember if she had ordered groceries. *No, that was yesterday.*

"Phoebe." Her name rattled through the door, through the headphones, cutting crisp and clear. Shying away despite recognizing the voice, Phoebe debated not opening the door. Maybe she'd turn the music back up and feign ignorance.

Curiosity won out in the end.

"Just a moment. The lock is sticking." The lie came easily and fell sharp from her lips as she placed her hands, one on the knob, one on the lock. She breathed in, out, and in again. She'd recognized that inflection on her name, knew who stood on the other side of the door. For a moment, maybe three, she hesitated again and debated leaving it locked.

Leaving it closed, leaving the night uninterrupted, leaving her domicile undisturbed and sealed against the outside world.

"Open the door." The words, crystal clear despite the thick slab of wood between her and the outside, between the inside and her headphones. A loud clarion call, enough to make Phoebe wince under its onslaught.

She turned the lock and reached for the chain, hesitating before leaving it fastened. It gave her enough room to open the door. She did so, but only at a slight crack. Not peeking out, she used the door like a shield.

"What is it now?" Phoebe's voice was quiet, hesitant, but no less steely for it. "We're not due to meet for another two weeks, Tarly. You know my rules."

Tarly pressed a hand against the door, enough to apply just barely enough pressure to let Phoebe know she was there, as if there could be any doubt. "There's been an emergency."

"I don't know—"

"M has gone off the grid, hasn't been checking in and missed both their appointment and dead drop. Felix, well, he's not in the best state of mind right now. We're going to need you to check on something for us. We're not going to be able to get anyone else close enough, and you're going to have to help us out here. Help me out." The voice took on a softer tone, the shadow that coalesced through the crack of the door growing as the owner leaned in on the other side. "Listen, do this for me, for us, and we'll make certain you have income enough for the next six months. We'll stay out of your hair, nice and quiet like."

"You've said this before, Tarly."

"I know, Pheebs, I know. Trust me, I know. I mean it this time. We're in a hell of a bind. Can I count on you?" She used that tone, the one Phoebe regretted revealing as her weakness.

Hemming and hawing internally, Phoebe nodded despite being out of sight behind the door. "When?" She sighed, pulling it open just a scant bit more. Noise filtered in from all of the other apartments. Loud, jarring, invasive; the lives of other people collided into her quiet abode. She grimaced. Bit down on the inside of her cheek as she flipped the switch on her headphones, dialing up the outside-dampening feature.

"Thank you, Pheebs. Here." Despite the headphones, Tarly's voice reverberated loud and clear. *Too loud, too clear.*

Phoebe grit her teeth against it, cracking the door just enough for the thick manila envelope to fit through, which she grasped. From the space behind the envelope, a green eye peered at her.

Phoebe met that gaze. It pinned her where she stood, froze her for a moment before she could react. She managed to close the door and rested her forehead against the cold wooden slab. Her next breath caught in her throat, hitched, before she forcefully swallowed and tried to breathe again.

"Listen, Pheebs. Phee. Bee. Bo. Beep." A pause, before Tarly continued, "Ms. Phoebe. You'll be okay. I promise, for real this time. Just this one job, right?" She used that tone, almost wheedling, sweet to the point of being saccharine. Underlying the words loud enough for Phoebe to hear the unspoken debt that she owed. To Tarly.

Phoebe sighed, screwing her eyes shut. *What's the danger of one job?* She knew the answer to that question, and knew she should say no. But she couldn't. "Fine. I'll do it."

"I knew you would. Good Phoebe, good girl."

Though Phoebe couldn't see her, she pictured that smirk on her face, that knowing look, and it drove a shiver through her.

"Check in if you need to and...be careful."

Phoebe felt, more than heard, the worry in that statement, as it slammed into her like a towering, teetering wall. She swallowed hard again, and nodded, not that Tarly could see. She didn't have to look through the peephole to know the only thing on the other side of the door was Tarly's shadow cast from the hall light as she left.

Alone again, Phoebe thumbed on her music. Loud enough to make her wince. She fumbled with the locks and secured herself away from the outside world, clutching the manila envelope tight to her chest. Her fingers drummed against it, a slow, rhythmic counterpoint to the beat of her heart.

Phoebe paced the suddenly confining apartment as she let the music calm her back down. A custom mixture of waves and forest sounds, coupled with some of her favorite music, flooded her ears. The built-up anxiety cradled in her chest burst like a dam.

"Let's see what we have here." She set the envelope on her desk and began organizing it. Not that it was much of a mess, but she put everything in its place before she moved the manila folder. Right in front. Blank, no writing on the outside. Nothing to betray the mystery waiting inside.

Not that that mattered.

She sat down and withdrew her hand when one song ended and cross-faded into another, a heavy sigh escaping her lips. *One more job. Just one more.* Tarly's words, planted like a seed, grew quickly in the fertile soil of her mind, choking off the part of her that rebelled against the idea.

Picking up the envelope and flipping it over, she untwisted its cord and slipped her finger beneath the tape and worked it open. Two papers, loose on top of a bound dossier. Withdrawing those, setting the dossier aside as she took her recorder out of a drawer and clicked it on.

A zoomed-in photograph from a higher vantage point of a man in business casual clothing, nondescript, except for the cowlick of sandy-blond hair that stuck up from the back of his head. Through the long-distance zoom, not a detail was lost. Phoebe could see the fearful, furtive look on his face. She flipped the photograph over and reviewed the vital statistics.

"Elias T. Ballard. Age 32, blond hair, black eyes. Long face, no visible distinguishing marks."

Phoebe skipped over the rest of the physical profile meant for M, to the highlighted parts on the next paper meant for her.

"Works at an office building on the corner of 3rd and Amerige Avenue, routinely exits the building around 11:30 AM, usually to take a phone call while headed to the diner across the street. Need his ten code words, office protected by biometric scans."

Phoebe sighed, shaking her head a little as she warmed to the task at hand. "M, what happened to you? This job has your name written all over it. I hope you're okay, wherever you are." Biting her lip, she shoved down her worry. Phoebe shook her head again as she turned the recorder off. Her eyes moved back to the top of the paper, read over the statistics again, the target, the task. Again and again, until her eyelids grew too heavy.

Headphones firmly over her ears, and the noise-canceling set to max, Phoebe set her playlist to the loudest brown noise track and set it to loop before unlocking her door.

By the time she found herself in the hallway, where the noises of everyone and everything around her threatened to drive her right back in, it was already too late. She couldn't—*wouldn't*—turn back now. Tarly needed her. The loud roar of the track drove away most of the chitter-chatter and noise threatening to overwhelm her. She locked up and turned, drawing her coat tighter around herself as she adjusted her messenger bag on her shoulder.

"She's counting on us. We can do this, Phoebe. We have to." She could barely hear herself through the headphones as she took a step away from her apartment. The hallway stretched out before her, as did the pattern of door, light, door, light, only broken by the elevator in the middle before it continued.

Vertigo slammed into her as she stared at the other end of the hall, enough that she almost retreated back, back, back into the safety of her apartment. Into the quiet cocoon of her existence.

Tarly's words echoed in her head. *Good Phoebe, good girl.*

Phoebe smiled as the part of her that feared stepping out into the open after so long shriveled away to near nothing, overridden and overwhelmed by the part of her that came to life with every step she took into the world.

Before she could think twice, she pulled her phone out and switched from the current anxiety-reducing track of soothing noise to her exercise playlist. Rhythmic beats worked better with the anticipation that built in her chest, thrummed in her heart.

She whispered along with the opening track, Billie Eilish's *Bad Guy,* a giggle tittering halfway off of her lips. With the music came sounds from the apartments she passed as she strode toward the elevator, now mostly a dull murmur beneath her notice.

Mr. Caldwell and his angry muttering about the state of the world, and how in his day... Mr. Cook, and his loud worries about his colleague, and whether or not she'd actually tell his wife. Phoebe smirked at that, shaking her head. She pushed through the clamor from the other units and escaped into the relative silence of the elevator.

Silent, except for its rattling and squeaks, but even those provided some relief from the rest of the tenants. Striding into the lobby, where the loudness dwarfed even what came from the apartments, she lost herself in the music.

Phoebe continued singing the song to herself with the same low, throaty growl as Billie. She slipped her sunglasses on as she pressed out into the bright light of midday.

The streets provided some much-needed relief from the lobby's chaos, because while the streets were just as loud and noisy, everything moved by in whispers and whooshes, moving too fast for any one source to inundate her.

Phoebe paused long enough to type in the address of the office building on her GPS. Uptown, and a few blocks over. For a moment, she debated the subway, or calling for a cab, but being trapped in either scenario with too many people too close, or one person that much closer, set her teeth on edge.

Deciding to walk, Phoebe put her phone away again and let the music protect her as the GPS gave her directions.

Elias Ballard. 3rd and Amerige.

Affixing the image of Elias in her mind, she focused on that and not the people around her. A sea of faces, of voices, of a volume she hated, despised, shied away from on any other day. Today, though?

"I have a job to do. I'm a good girl," Phoebe said again, louder than she intended, and louder than she probably should have as it drew a handful of stares her way. Furtive, on her mission, she put on the air that she belonged exactly where she was. The little lady in her phone continued giving her directions.

Turn left here. Two blocks ahead, take a right. Continue on for six blocks.

Phoebe followed along with the voice prompts, her gaze locked ahead, on her target. The large building loomed in the distance, easy to see. Glancing at the time on her phone, she caught the minute just as it clicked over to 11:15 AM.

"If you're early, you're on time. If you're on time, you're late. And if you're late?" Phoebe *tsk*ed a few times, shuddering as memories of Retail Hell flooded back in, threatening to distract her from the task at hand. The building towered over a few others, with a communal courtyard and a fountain between them. Multiple food vendors had set up shop near the many benches.

Walking past the food trucks idling at the curb, Phoebe circled the courtyard twice before she found an empty bench away from everyone else which still offered a clear view of her target's building.

Elias Ballard. Focusing on his name as if she might summon him by chanting it in her head, Phoebe turned down the volume on her phone, trying to do just that. As if she were a kid again, waiting for her parents to pick her up, channeling every thought into making them appear. The music faded to the backdrop, and the noise of the world rushed in like water escaping a breaking dam. Gritting her teeth against the sheer amount of noise assaulting her, she turned her mind as blank as she could. She practiced breathing in, out, in, out, locking her attention on the doors ahead and nothing else.

"Focus, Phoebe. You can do this. You *have* to." Nodding to herself, she turned the music back up a little bit, drowning out the world to a low, dull roar. Her gaze occasionally flitted away from the doors as people walked past her, wisps and noises of their lives trying to distract her. She bit her lip, closed her eyes, breathed, and forced herself to look back at the doors.

Only blinking when her eyes demanded it, Phoebe watched as the trickle of people coming and going swelled into a much larger crowd, filling the corporate courtyard. She briefly wondered what a large group of people might be called. A herd, for cows, a murder, for crows. Not a flock, like birds, even if some of them flapped their arms animatedly while yelling into the phone.

Something caught her attention.

There.

Elias Ballard.

Phoebe squeaked as the intonation of his name in her mind drew his gaze right to her. Or so she feared, as he walked with apparent purpose toward her, she held her breath. Had he found her out already? She squeaked again as he neared, and only remembered how to breathe as he passed right by her. Unable to fight the urge to turn and watch, Phoebe tittered again, realizing she had practically sat right in front of the diner.

"Silly Pheebs. Silly, silly Phoebe." Muttering aloud, turning around on her bench, she readjusted and, as nonchalantly as she could, she affected a comfortable perch on the bench while focusing her gaze on her mark.

Elias Ballard. Repeating his name, she concentrated on him as he sat, peering at the menu. Standing, Phoebe took a zig-zagging path closer toward the diner, towards her quarry.

Elias. A spark jolted through her, from her head to her toe and back again, causing her to grin.

"I got you dead to rights. Wake up." Phoebe took a seat at a bench nearer the diner and turned the music off, ignoring the few concerned looks shot her way. The world, waiting in the wings, rushed back in and doubled down. She pulled her headset down, resting them around her neck.

Phoebe winced at the din. *So loud.* Her heart raced, her breath hitched, but she kept her attention firmly upon her target.

Elias Ballard.

T.

Elias T. Ballard.

This close, his presence screamed loudest of all to her. That, at least, helped her focus and filter out everything—no, everyone else. The world around her blurred, darkening at the edges, as *Elias* became her everything. The rest fell away, all of the many distractions, noises becoming a low, dull buzzing at the edge of her senses.

I see you, Phoebe thought as she relaxed, letting her eyes drift closed, blocking out visual distractions. And she did see him.

There, in her mind's eye, Elias T. Ballard stood as plain as day, surrounded by naught but darkness. The same darkness Phoebe conjured and retreated to when the world became too much. When she needed to do nothing but think, remember. Process. *Explore.*

"Hello, Elias," Phoebe whispered to the shape of him in her head, her voice quiet enough anyone walking by wouldn't hear. "What are you hiding?" Her words echoed in that nowhere space, reverberating enough to surround him.

Remaining where she sat on the bench, a piece of her stood in the confines of her mind, moving to better investigate his specter.

"You're lonely. You're scared. It's okay, Pheebs is here." Without moving from her seat, she reached out, her eyes closed tight against the world. Even with her focus completely on the job, the world threatened to chip away at her calm, her resolve. "Just a little push. A prod. Ah, yes. There we go." She hummed happily to herself, smiling slightly as the picture of Elias spoke.

"Jury."

Good Pheebs. Tarly's words came back to her as she blushed, and she pushed a little harder. As much as the world tried to remind her of its pervasive presence, all of those other people and their noisome lives, she turned that energy inward, against Elias.

The image of him spoke again. *"News. Norm. Keep."* Three more words in quick, rapid-fire succession formed eagerly on his lips.

A drop of sweat broke out on her forehead. A warm sensation dribbled and trickled against her lip. "Careful, Phoebe. Careful," she whispered, admonishing herself as she withdrew. A headache started chipping at her awareness, a lightning-quick strike of pain lancing through her head, down her spine. Without thinking, she dabbed at her nose with a handkerchief, red to hide the blood. Sighing and breathing deep, she pressed on.

Deeper.

"Give me more, Elias T. Ballard."

"Accident. Evaluate. Arm. Consult—" The spectral man turned his head to her with a piercing gaze.

Shit. Phoebe withdrew, the taste of anxiety creeping into the back of her throat. The world rushed over the erected dam, reminding her of its existence.

"Ma'am, are you okay?" A voice, close, concerned—too close, too concerned—drew Phoebe further from herself and from *Elias.*

Peeking with one eye, she stared at the form leaning over her. After her eyes adjusted to the daylight once more, it resolved itself into a uniformed cop. Her pale blue eyes regarded Phoebe with worry, her hand on her radio.

Swallowing hard and dabbing again at the bloody nose with her handkerchief, Phoebe tried to speak. The words caught in her throat as a spike of fear pinned her in place. Refusing to give in to the rising panic, she managed a small nod while trying to find her voice. "I, uh, I'm fine." Stammering, Phoebe offered a smile, wan at best, trying to keep *Elias* centered in her mind while torn between her worlds, the real one, and the one in her mind. "Allergies, and my apartment, it's so dry. I'm out here to get some fresh air, and, oh, I'm fine. Please. Please don't worry about me." Phoebe tried to put more into the smile, staring hard at the officer.

The cop narrowed her eyes, doubt radiating on her face.

Before Phoebe could stop herself, she narrowed her own eyes. With a light—featherlight but nevertheless insistent—reaching of her mind, she sought out the officer's. *Go away. Please and thank you.*

Bam. Just like that, the officer blinked, shrugged, and walked away.

Phoebe shut her eyes again. When she found herself alone in that dim room, panic threatened to set in once more. She screwed her eyes shut tighter, chewing on her lip as she searched. There, Elias stood, a shadow within the corner of her mind. After a moment of forcing herself to concentrate, and another stab of pain, his wavering, dissipating form slammed back into focus.

Phoebe gritted her teeth, once more blanking out the outside world.

Elias T. Ballard. 32. Long face. His face, or her perception of it, became clearer, down to every follicle of stubble of skin not shaved for days. Sweat on his brow, fear in his eyes. His emotions roiled in them, and she sensed they threatened to wash over her, glimpses of more just beneath the surface.

Ten secrets, all in all, with three remaining. She dug in once more. *"Consultation. Fish. Plain."*

A grimace of pain fluttered through Elias's specter, his face tw*isting in a rictus of agony. His mouth opened and words flooded out before she could stop them.* "They said this is perfectly safe, that I just have to babysit this building, this floor, this chamber. Can I know what's in it, at least? Oh, no, that's above my paygrade. At least it pays well. I can get that jet ski I've always dreamed of. Still, something seems off. I'm starting to see people lurking by the building."

That part of Phoebe that hated this, hated her using these powers, tried to rear its head once more. Something about that stream of consciousness scared her, deep down inside, with the implication of what might happen to Elias T. Ballard now that she stole the passcodes. The concern sat deep enough that she could—and did—ignore it. With her mission complete, and the ten words safely in her possession, Phoebe started to dismantle her connection to Elias.

And yet, something lingered there, a thought, a curiosity in her. What *was* he protecting?

She leaned closer, her presence overbearing in Elias's mind. She felt him recoil, his mind shuttering against her attempts to find that information.

Information he, apparently, didn't actually have. And yet, Elias did fear *something*, though, in spades. That gave Phoebe momentary pause as her concern grew.

What had Tarly gotten her into?

She couldn't resist digging further as she drank it all in. Gulped at it, as she rearranged the room within her mind so that, from her front row seat, she could watch his simulacrum twisted this way and that, betraying his cool, cold exterior she'd spied in the diner.

The scene before her changed from Elias standing, reacting to her every poke and prod, to a television set large enough to cover one of her apartment walls. Each screen displayed Elias at different moments of his life, a loop of memories.

"Let's see what else you have lurking in here, boyo." Phoebe bit her lip, sat down on the couch across from the giant TV, and pointed the remote suddenly in her hand. "Let's see what's on, oh. Hmm." Pressing buttons, the television flared to life as titled memories appeared for her viewing pleasure.

Every facet of Elias moved in slow motion across its portion of the screen, snippets of his life ready at a button's touch.

"What have you been hiding?"

Hungry to know—to *see*—exactly what Elias hid, besides the secret code comprised of ten words. Clips of his life played out, and she surfed through the options. From a failed date from his college days to when he nearly fainted giving a presentation about rain forests in seventh-grade science class.

Phoebe giggled, leaning over as she flipped through her own personal reality television.

Until the signal grew staticky before giving out completely.

Shocked back into her body, into the uncomfortably hard bench in the corporate courtyard, Phoebe blinked against the return of harsh sunlight. She looked around, trying to remember where she was, and it took a few moments to piece everything back together.

She spotted Elias standing there, not in the diner but in the courtyard, holding his head. The look of confusion, pain, clear on his face made her swallow. Hard. She hated feeling those feelings not her own.

After gathering himself, Elias headed back into his building.

A frown tugged at the edge of her lips. "Not so fast, Phoebe Bee Bo Beeps," she murmured to herself, leaving her headphones around her neck. She pulled out her phone and let her fingers dance across the screen. The haptic feedback seemed loud as she texted the ten code words to Tarly with a sunglasses smiley emoji and a thumbs up.

"Okay, job's done." Breathing deep, she started to put the headphones on, planning to leave.

But the cacophony of so many people with so many problems drew her attention. What would another little glimpse hurt? Not *her*. Sure, some of them might get headaches, maybe some nightmares, but that was a small price for them to pay. Licking her lips, and biting down on the lower, she gazed at all of the people still gathered, either reading a book or simply soaking up the sunlight. Those who bustled to and fro provided quick glimpses while she felt out her next target ripe for the plucking.

"Let's see who else is on the boob tube." Her eyes moved up, hunger in her gaze, as she found one of the food vendors. Nowhere near as careful as she had been with Elias and digging for his secret words, she dove in, eager to see someone else's life. Searching for the pain, the misery, she reached in and found herself in that dark room, on the couch, an entire life on display.

"I've missed this," Phoebe said, before another giggle escaped as she hit play.

THE HIDDEN COST

NIKHAIL. PROBLEM. NEED YOU at HHCH right fucking now. Yesterday even. Room 1408, I'll get everything situated.

Nikhail stared at the message sitting unread on his phone, the notification showing him that someone, somewhere, needed him. The problem? It seemed like everyone, everywhere, needed him. Or nigh enough that it hardly mattered trying to figure out an accurate number.

The cold press of a gun against the back of his head drew his attention back to matters at hand. Swallowing hard, his eyes flicked away from the phone.

Noticing his distraction, a large hand reached and took it out of his field of view.

"You really don't need to do that. Please." Nikhail kept his voice calm, doing his best to sit very, very still. One flinch, and his brains might splatter all over the room if the goon at his back pulled the trigger, accidentally or otherwise.

"Word on the street is that you help people, Nikky." Words, with an accent Nikhail could not quite place, from behind him. Harsh, mirroring the press of the circular nozzle of the gun pressed against his skin. That, at least, served to distract him from the solid slab of an oak desk in front of him that had been, somehow, dragged to the middle of the room. And from the huddled mass of flesh sprawled on top of it, soaking what was once a pristine surface with blood.

The stench of copper and sweat filled the room, as did the incessant low groaning of someone in pain. A lot of pain. There were others in there, standing in the wings, keeping their distance, never letting their hands stray far from the conspicuously inconspicuous bulges in their poorly tailored jackets.

One last visitor hovered nearby, invisible, intangible, but Nikhail knew Death when it came near. Everyone looked at Nikhail. He felt the weight of every beady eye turned his way, almost as heavy as the weight of the gun.

Swallowing hard, trying to moisten the desert in his mouth, Nikhail didn't move more than he had to as he spoke. "Listen. Yes. Okay? You're right, I help people. But—"

"Then help Mr. Massucci. Hurry." As if to punctuate the meaning of the voice behind Nikhail, the figure on the table groaned that much louder as he writhed in agony, his screams soon cut short with a gurgle as he collapsed again.

Nikhail winced. *Mr. Massucci?* His brain processed a mile a minute, trying to remember where he heard that name before. *Oh, fuck. Fuck a duck, and screw a kangaroo, this isn't good, buddy-boo. This is Terenzio 'The Terminator' Massucci.* Nikhail gulped again, hard, trying not to panic. At least, to not panic more than he already was. Any advice his therapist had given him flew right out the window as anxiety, fear, and everything in-between flooded into him.

"Look, I get it. You want me to help—"

"Want has nothing to do with it. You want to walk out of here without broken kneecaps, or *at all,* you're going to do everything you can to fix this up. Right and proper, hear me?" The gun pressed harder against his head.

Nikhail could already feel the bruise forming. "You don't understand. First, fucking stop poking me with the gun like this is prom night and we're slow dancing with the chaperone looking the other way. It's not going to help anything. For fuck's sake." He'd lost control of his mouth, half expecting that to be the moment everything went black. Forever.

When his mouth failed to get him killed, he pressed his luck.

"You're half right. Sure, I can help people. I'm not going to lie my way around that one. I'm not keen on that as it is. Nor am I going to be able to do what you want. Not the way you think." Nikhail drew a breath in and held it.

"You assume you have a choice in this matter, I see." A growl.

A cocking of the, what's that part called? The knobber? The hammer? Either way, it made him flinch.

"You assume you know what the flying fuck you're talking about. I cannot do what you want, the way you want." Nikhail grimaced, knowing his words would fall on ignorant ears. "There's a price to pay for my help." He tried to keep his voice at least *somewhat* steady, even if his heart raced all over the place.

"Wake up, Nikky. Don't be greedy now." The voice's owner moved from around behind him, and what little reprieve granted by the gun moving from gouging into the back of Nikhail's head went away just as quick as it loomed so close to his forehead, his eyes had to cross to stare down its dark chamber. That meant one thing. Death was knocking. Maybe it'd be a quick one. Hopefully a quick one.

Nikhail's mouth got away from him again. "Greed has nothing to do with it, you dolt." Clamping it shut, forcing his eyes to look past the slight sway of the gun barrel so very close, he looked at the giant chunk of muscle that held the gun in a meaty hand.

Bald, a nose broken countless times, skinny lips, hard eyes. Sharp edges and bulk, wrapped in flesh, and a suit marginally better than the other goons.

"If I don't miss my mark, if that's Mr. Massucci on the table, and you're the most vocal one here, that must make you, what is it? Either Gavin 'Buster' Boitano, or Cael 'Good Looking' Pocklington. And unless that's one of those names like 'Tiny' for a man that's decidedly not, I'm going to go with Buster."

The man narrowed his eyes, nodding as he spoke. "Funny words from a funny man one wisecrack away from death's door."

"Buster, then." Nikhail swallowed hard, watching the man nod. "Okay, good, Buster, buddy? Listen, listen real good like. You know what I can do, that's why we're in this predicament. That's also why *you* had to come to *me*. I'm not out here doing this shit because it's good for my health, or anyone else's, really."

"What are you spouting off? We need you to do this. Boss-man will make it worth your while, see," Buster grunted, gesturing with his gun.

"Yes, but you see what the whispers don't get right? There's a cost. A hidden cost. There's always a price to pay, to balance the scales, so to speak." Nikhail drew a deep breath. He *knew* what the next words out of Buster's mouth would be. This is how it always began.

"Boss man has money, you greedy fuck," Buster growled.

"If only it were that easy. I'd be the richest man in the damn world and a messiah to boot. No, what people fail to mention in the afterglow of having their lives saved, is they rarely understand the cost. And here, because I really don't feel like learning what a lead-based implant will feel like, I'm going to be straight with you. This isn't about money; this isn't about greed. This is, well, *whatever* the fuck this is. I can't just waggle my fingers and poof, someone has a new spleen, or *bam!* They can walk again." Nikhail shook his head.

Buster's eyes widened a little, perhaps realizing how out of his depth he was. "What, then?"

"Someone has to pay a price. An eye for an eye, so to speak. If you want Mr. Massucci to see tomorrow, if this is really, truly that dire—and by the way, he's gone three more shades of pale in the time that it's taken you get yourself nice and hard with that gun—I'd say time's real short. That means we're already on borrowed minutes. Hours at best." Nikhail drew another deep breath, wincing at his own words. He hated them, because this went against every single thing in his Hippocratic Oath. He wanted nothing more than to help, and with his power, he couldn't. Not without a cost. He continued before Buster could get his mouth to work, "It's not literally an eye for an eye, not always, no. He's been, what, shot? A few times?" He perched a little higher in his chair for a better vantage point. "That means someone has a choice to make. Either they offer their body up to take on some of the damage, the pain, or give a bit of themselves. Something they cherish. Can you do that, Buster? Any of you? Will you trade your life for his?"

Buster avoided the look Nikhail shot him, and the rest of the goons looked everywhere but at him.

That got the point home, at least. He paused, letting a few precious seconds tick away, until a full minute of what little time the Terminator had left ceased to be.

None of them spoke up, not a one. Which did not surprise him at all.

"See? That's a price most are unwilling to pay. I get that. Life is precious, and all that. Our own, the most of all." He tried to smile before finally standing up, quite certain no one was going to shoot him, least of all the busted Buster standing in front of him. "All that said and done, if you'd let me proceed?"

No one spoke, and Buster finally lowered his damn arm, holstering the gun beneath his jacket before smoothing it down.

Nikhail stepped closer to Mr. Massucci, still groaning and wavering in and out of consciousness. "I see you doped him up. Okay, not ideal, really not ideal, but I guess I get it. Squeals of pain are going to draw attention, and we don't want that. Not at this critical juncture." He spoke more for his own sake than for the goons', carefully inspecting Mr. Massucci. Someone had already cut away most of his clothing, done some sort of rudimentary digging for bullets in holes. Nikhail glanced sideways and saw a little dish full of twisted, crimson-stained metal fragments.

More than he would have anticipated.

"Shit." He breathed the word out, under his breath. Not that it mattered in the quiet room. He held up his hand as Buster stepped forward, and shook his head. "I got this. Maybe."

"What about the cost?" Buster spoke through gritted teeth. Obviously that subject still smarted.

"We'll get there. Patience, young grasshopper." Ignoring the grunt from Buster, Nikhail touched Mr. Massucci's clammy and sweaty forehead, hovering his other hand over the shoddy bandages across Massucci's midsection, already bleeding through.

Nikhail could feel each and every wound as if they were his own. And after a fashion, they were. He felt the torn flesh, lacerations on deeper parts of his body. All of it rushed in, the perforated spleen, to bile leaking out of a ruptured stomach. He could *almost* smell the contents of the torn intestines. Such was the price of his connection to Mr. Massucci's broken body.

He hated this part; feeling the pain, the torment, the torture, and knowing he could help. Had to help, even if a bullet didn't have his name on it. He had taken an oath even before all of this, to help those who needed it.

Never thought it'd work out like this, he thought with a slight chuckle.

"What's so funny, funny man?"

"Certainly not your propensity for the words 'funny' and 'man,' but nothing. Not a single damn thing is remotely funny about this, and I find myself prone to chuckling nervously as I wonder if I'll even see tomorrow should I manage to pull this off. That's all besides the point, though. If you keep interrupting me with these inane—no, I'll say it—downright *stupid* questions, I'd almost think *you wanted* me to fail. Is that it?" Nikhail spat the last words out.

Buster paled and vehemently shook his head.

Delving back into the shitshow of Mr. Massucci's massacred, mangled, and maimed internal organs, Nikhail closed his eyes against the room, the distractions of Buster and his gun, and felt the thread attached to every wound, to him, through him. Each one, a tally to be paid that he both felt and saw, and it made him sick. All threads ended at a gaping, hungry maw waiting to consume the price paid to heal these many wounds. Ripping and tearing, devouring what people held dear, a trade for healing.

In exchange for what? A life, in this instance. Two, if Nikhail's were to be counted, and he really hoped so. He was trapped in this room, with the only way out, the only way to save himself, tied with healing the monster on the table. And yet, how much harm might he cause by doing this, by saving this gangster? Trapped between a rock and a hard place, with this *need* to consume, to right these mortal-coil wrongs. To stave off Death, and who knew for how long?

With every second that ticked, every blood droplet that dripped, the cost increased.

The price to be paid. A voice, not necessarily his own, though not necessarily not.

Nikhail followed the threads attached to each wound, a series of price tags to heal. He ignored the part ingrained into him: *do no harm*. If he could help someone, and if they knew the cost, what harm was there, truly?

As he focused, the prices trailed off into the distance, to the life-forces in the room. Buster, the other goons, all viable sources. But this power reached even further, to Mr. Massucci's daughter, a virtuoso on the violin, or Buster's cousin, who had a way with numbers. The choice remained in Nikhail's hands. Mr. Massucci's heart stopped, but only because time itself solidified around Nikhail as he bargained for life.

A life not his own, but one to which he was inextricably linked.

Taking from others was somehow, unfairly, that much more powerful. Each of the men in the room had someone in their family that shone bright. Brighter than these men, that's for certain, and thus, the power drew itself towards them.

No. Nikhail drew it back in, fighting it. *Not them.*

The price to be paid? A question, radiating eagerness, ravenous, turning on Nikhail. Would it truly turn on him?

Daring not to think about it, he turned his attention back to the men in the room. Inspiration struck. Time unfroze as he drew in the payments without any further thought, putting his mind and his power to work on Mr. Massucci's innards, wielding them as deftly as any scalpel he ever held.

Sweat dripped over his brow as Nikhail glanced at the desk clock thrown on the floor. Even upside down, he wondered where the last thirty minutes went. Somewhere, in the background, the goons filtered in and out of the room. Shadows in the dark, each one unwittingly bringing *something* to the table as the guard changed. How many times, he had no idea. Nikhail felt the hunger inside himself, lost himself in it, and all too gladly fed it, closing his eyes against all distractions.

Until nothing else needed suturing. Nothing major, at least. Almost every little wrong turned right, fixed.

Nikhail shuddered as the power left him empty. With a stuttering breath, he opened his eyes once more.

Buster stared him down.

Surprisingly enough, so did Mr. Massucci, prone on the desk, his head canted ever so slightly to the side.

"Wha—" Mr. Massucci started, but Buster placed a hand on his shoulder.

"Don't go stressing yourself none. Nikky here fixed you up proper." Buster helped Mr. Massucci to his feet, with the latter giving an appraising glance toward Nikhail, whose skin shivered at that.

Mr. Massucci waved Buster away as he turned to face Nikhail, straightening his blood-stained clothing as if it mattered. "We could use a...man...like you."

"You aren't the only one." Nikhail grimaced, shaking his head as he tried to wipe his hands clean of the entire affair.

"Smart boy like you needs to play his cards right. Get taken care of." Mr. Massucci somehow, even having been just on death's door, managed to loom in the suddenly small room, his voice quiet yet forceful. His steely gray gaze lanced Nikhail where he stood.

"Listen. Your goons knew where to find me, but try to not get yourself nearly dead, and they won't have to do so again." He drew a deep breath and fought the urge to blow it right back out just as fast. His tongue itched to get snarky but didn't dare. "If I might take my leave?"

"Go, but you'll be hearing from—maybe even seeing—us again, Nikky boy." Buster handed him back his phone before waving him on.

Nikhail took that opportunity to get the absolute fuck out of the room as quickly as he could. Near tripping over himself, around the desk, until he had to edge past the two burly guards at the door and the miasma of cheap cologne that clouded them. Ignoring the other men outside, and the sickly yellow lights casting the hallway in a gut-wrenching color, he hid his shaking hands in his pocket, stepping toward the elevator.

Against his better judgment, he glanced over his shoulder.

Mr. Massucci stood at the door, swaying ever so slightly, tattered clothes stained with blood, pale flesh on display, free of defects. Mr. Massucci, who prized his business acumen, ruthlessness, and negotiation skills above everything else. Behind him, Buster, whose unparalleled strength made him the muscle of the crew, and with his smarts? That made him the top lieutenant. Then there were the other men, those who knew the best contacts on the street, with their network of eyes and ears. One had a boyhood friend in the police force, oft prone to getting drunk and talkative. Another—and this hurt the most of all—had the most delectable of pie recipes.

Those were almost enough for the cost, but not quite.

The price required sacrifice, hungered for more. So much more. Nikhail did the best he could, stealing what each thug loved most. A friendship that would sour, a recipe that would never quite turn out right again, and an empire of crime and threats that would slowly crumble like the bad cookies his grandmama always called the 'ne'er-do-wells.'

But the power wanted—*needed*—more. Nikhail had refused to let it extend to innocent people and corralled it in the room with him and the goons. All that remained, laid out plainly on the table, was the camaraderie. Loyalty. These, the power supped on eagerly to heal Mr. Massucci.

He turned away from Mr. Massucci's glare, refusing to look over his shoulder again as the elevator dinged, the door sliding open. He stepped in and only then, as he was forced to turn around, did he dare look.

Mr. Massucci stood in a heated conversation with Buster, the two arguing about something. Whatever words they exchanged tapered off as the office door slammed.

Someone screamed, the sound punctuated by the explosive blast of a gunshot.

Ducking into the corner of the elevator as another shot rang out, Nikhail slammed the *Door Close* button repeatedly, thankful the elevator listened.

On the ride down, he couldn't help but breathe a little easier the further he descended, away from the unfolding chaos.

The price, sometimes, well...sometimes it outweighed the benefit.

He entertained no doubts Mr. Massucci and Buster figured that out. But too late.

Stepping out of the elevator as it opened, Nikhail's phone exploded with notifications loud enough to make him jump half out of his skin. Fumbling the thing out of his pocket, he stared at the notification bar, so full of messages, all he saw was the red exclamation point where a number should be. Nikhail thumbed through them, a sigh building hard and heavy in his chest.

Please, you're the only one who can help us. We'll pay anything.
You greedy bastard.
Fuck you!

Please please please please.

All variations on the same thing, until he got to one of the latest messages.

Nikhail. Problem. Need you at HHCH right fucking now. Yesterday even. Room 1408, I'll get everything situated.

Enid. A small smile flitted over his lips at that as he thumbed back a response. *BRT.* Hitting send, Nikhail kept dismissing the notifications until another one caught his eye.

Report in.

Where are you?

This isn't funny.

Don't bite the hand that feeds you, Nikhail.

Each and every one of them from Darlie, different variations looking for a report. Looking for him. Sighing, he put himself on autopilot as he walked through the city, wishing for nothing more than as much distance between him and that building as possible.

Shuddering as the adrenaline wore off, Nikhail forced himself to thumb out a response to his handler.

(N.) Seems I am a very popular man tonight. Caught some attention but it's been dealt with. I'm going to need a new number, too. This one's compromised.

(Darlie) ....

(Darlie) AGAIN? What the fuck did you do? You're supposed to be laying low, nice and quiet like!

(Darlie) You have no idea how loudly I just rolled my eyes.

(Darlie) Seriously, fill me in on the deets.

(N.) I'm fine, Darlie.

(Darlie) Okay, now you're worrying me. You're fine, good, dandy. What the hell happened?

(N.) You know the East-Street Elders?

(Darlie) NIKKY WHAT THE FUCK DID YOU DO

(N.) Yeah, they snatched me when I left to get a pizza earlier.

(Darlie) I TOLD YOU TO LAY LOW WHAT THE FUCK

(N.) Listen. I needed to get out and get some air. I've been cooped up too long. I might have helped someone along the way. Poor kid. And Enid needs me.

(Darlie) I thought she might reach out. Jazzy's in bad shape. Think you can find a way?

(N.) Probably. I'm headed there now.

(Darlie) Just get back to the safe house after this. I'll have a new burner waiting there for you. Dump that one.

(N.) Yes ma'am. And some pizza?

(Darlie) ....fine.

Nikhail smirked a little as he powered the phone off, twisted it in half. The first bit, he threw into the first trash can he passed. He waited more than a few blocks before he ditched the rest of it. He drew his hood over his head, trying to drown out the sounds of the city, the pain that practically radiated off of it, begging for his help, and headed for HHCH.

Previously On...

T HE STENCH OF STALE coffee and staler smoke filled the room, and if the yellowed walls were any indication, no one had even bothered to scrub them down since the smoking ban went into full effect. Carly paced the tight confines of the room, ignoring the hulking figure sitting at the desk in the middle. He wore a suit that looked like it might have been in vogue a few decades ago, likely never fit right in the first place, and had never seen the warm touch of an iron.

Ignoring the detective, Carly turned and stared at her reflection in the mirror, adjusting the collar of her shirt and the tie that threatened to choke her. Between the fabric at her throat and how very stifling the room temperature grew with every passing minute, she felt lightheaded. Breathing in tepid air, her head spun; her heart thundered loud enough in her chest, she swore that her reflection in the mirror vibrated enough to be fuzzy at the edges.

"Ms. Dunn. Arlene, if I may? Please, have a seat." A heavy voice, raspy and tired, drew her attention away from the two-way mirror and whatever shadowy figure lurked on the other side.

Carly could see when they fidgeted, maybe from foot to foot, waiting for the interrogation to start. "Detective Stedman, I told you, I have nothing to say until my lawyer arrives." She hated the tremor in her voice, turned away from the mirror after fixing a few locks of her hair, tucking the wild and errant strand of red that always escaped from the bun, or ponytail, or whatever.

"I understand that. Which is why I'm not asking you to say anything. Just sit down. Otherwise, you're liable to wear a hole in the linoleum, and the budget's already tight this year." Detective Stedman tried to smile through his joke, but the attempt was just as poor. He sighed again, shaking his head as he flipped the manila folder around to face her, as if to entice her back to the table. "See, I figured you might want to see this picture. Of you. Standing over the corpse."

"Allegedly." Carly stepped toward the table. The screech her chair emitted as she dragged it under herself made the detective sigh again. She leaned over as if to study the picture. "You think that's me?"

"Think? I'm pretty damn sure I know it is. You need to wake up to the trouble you're in, Ms. Dunn." Detective Stedman smirked, leaning back in his chair as he held his hands out. "Work with me here."

"Even with the shoddy quality, I can tell you that's not me. I wouldn't even be caught dead in such a gaudy coat, let alone photographed. As if." Carly pointed at the picture, before picking it up and studying it closer. "That's not me." Sweat trickled between her shoulder blades. She fought to keep her face straight. "Anyway, what did my lawyer say? When will they be here?"

His words came through lips pressed so tight together, they lost all color. "We can sort this out before your lawyer arrives, Ms. Dunn."

"You know very well that is *not* how this works, Detective." The words started out muffled and came that much clearer as someone thrust the door open. "I am her lawyer, and I am here, and that's all you need to know for the moment."

Carly did her best not to blink, staring at the lady standing in the doorway as if she owned the joint. Nary a hair or piece of clothing out of place, not like the usual tired, worn-down public defender she expected. Yet, the way the lawyer stood on the threshold of the interrogation room, Carly half expected her to vibrate into the room with the overflowing, pent-up energy.

Detective Stedman opened his mouth before the lawyer cut him off. "Ms. Dunn and I will be allowed our time to confer. Then, and only then, may this absolute farce that only the generous could call a line of questioning resume."

"Ah, I see." The detective cleared his throat but could not hide the growl of frustration from leaking out. Stedman narrowed his eyes. "Adelyn Nitz is your lawyer. I should've guessed."

Carly looked between them, their history growing palpable.

After a few moments of glaring in a silent contest of wills, someone knocked on the other side of the mirror. This broke Detective Stedman's attention. Carly watched the smirk widen on the lawyer's face as the detective's shoulders slumped.

"You've been summoned. Give us the room, please, and thank you. Right now. Get. Go." Adelyn shooed the detective out of his chair, and straight out of the room. Only once the door closed did she turn back, rolling her eyes. "About damn time. I swear." Adelyn sat on the chair, adjusting her blazer and skirt, immaculate and well pressed, as if they had somehow been crumpled. Setting her briefcase on the table, she flipped it open and started sorting through papers, waiting.

Carly swallowed, started to open her mouth, but Adelyn raised her hand and gave the faintest shake of her head. Biting her lip, swallowing her words back down, Carly relaxed into the uncomfortable embrace of her chair once more, even if the effort was doomed from the start. She looked up to the camera trained on them, the red light blinking in a steady pattern.

The light dimmed, went dark, and failed to come back on. Only then did Adelyn speak.

"Ms. Dunn. Arlene. I am your lawyer, Adelyn Nitz. Is it safe to assume that you know exactly why I am here with you, today?" She shuffled through the paperwork in her briefcase again before centering Carly in her gaze.

She blinked. "Because I am due a public defender?" Even as she spoke, the words felt off, felt wrong. The lady sitting across from her carried none of the usual wear and tear the job usually brought. The laugh Adelyn answered with rang to the truth of that, and how very wrong her own answer had been.

"No. To put it as bluntly as I can, so you understand me: I am here because you fucked up. Bad. Plain and simple, that's all there is to it. You're in some pretty hot water. And I represent, shall we say, an interested party who would rather see your particular skill set put to much better use than rotting away. Or dealing with petty revenge." Adelyn fanned out a series of photos. The quality of these put the detective's photos, temporarily shoved off to the side, to shame.

Carly spread them out a little more as if to study them, as if she didn't recognize her face splayed across the table, staring back at her, or just out of frame, unaware. "Are you trying to scare me with these?" She tried to laugh it off but hiccupped instead.

A burble of fear made itself known in her stomach as she stared at a series of photos of her. All dated at the same time, but in different parts of the city, different outfits. Biting her lip, Carly touched one of the photos, drawing it out where she could get a better look at her haggard face, drawn thin and tired.

"That's not me," she whispered, as if afraid someone else might hear.

Adelyn just stared at her, a knowing look on her smug face.

Carly curled her other hand into a fist beneath the table until her nails dug into the tender, meaty part of her palm. The pain helped her focus as the instinct to either fight or flee reared its ugly head. With nowhere to go, the need to lash out became that much worse, but she pushed it down. Breathed in, out, holding in between each and repeating.

"What do you want me to say? Obviously, these aren't me," she said, hoping the attempted nonchalance paid off.

"Let's get one thing straight right off the bat: do not play dumb with me, sweetheart. Not here, not now, not when it's wasting my time. You can do that with the detective all day long but understand that I would rather not be here. My employer has given you the grace of my help, and is paying for my time here, but not at the cost of you pressing my fucking buttons." Adelyn leaned over the table, hissing in frustration.

"Previously on the table, you had one chance to play smart. Do not screw up again. Got it?"

Carly blinked, leaning backward enough she nearly tipped her chair. "Ooookay." She looked at the photos again, before dragging her gaze away from the many facets of her face to look at Adelyn. "How are you going to help me?"

"Let me worry about that. But understand I do not come for free." Her expression held a threatening edge.

Carly swallowed her words, wondering what thoughts ran through the lawyer's head. Her own mind ran as she squirmed in her chair. Any time she opened her mouth to speak, Adelyn shot her a look that read, *Think twice before you speak.* Each time, Carly closed her mouth again. Her attention fell back to the pictures on the table, clearly her, her face, certain, but she had not entirely lied, either. Not completely. But still, it left her wondering exactly what the lawyer knew, or how much. Looking at the dates on the photos, all the same but taken at different places, spoke to what the lawyer might know.

"What do you want from me?" she asked, wincing at the squeak in her voice.

"You are a person of interest to my employer." Adelyn looked at her nails, picking at them, before making a pointed look at her watch.

Carly read the message loud and clear. Time, and the lawyer's patience, ran thin. "And if I say no?" she blurted. And immediately recoiled from the disparaging look Adelyn levied at her. Remaining silent, she tried to figure another way out of this mess, another answer to this problem, one better than the vice-grip on her.

Meanwhile, Adelyn looked at her phone and busied herself with sending messages as if she didn't have a care in the world.

And why would she? Carly thought, her heart stammering in her chest. *She couldn't care less. But what other choice do I have?* Her mind latched onto that. Even with the unknown of it, something—*anything*—had to be better than dealing with the detective, who had her dead to rights.

Still uncertain, but knowing her options to get off of this sinking ship were limited, Carly nodded "I'm in," she whispered.

"Good. Leave this to me. We will be in touch after this. Now sit there, shut up, look pretty, and let me do what I do best." Adelyn set her phone down, not even bothering to look at Carly before reaching to knock on the door, summoning the detective.

Bright sunlight blinded Carly, making her blink even as she tried to shield her eyes with her hand, trying to adjust to the outside world after being cooped up in the dim building. In the small interrogation room whose stench seemed to still cling to her, filled her nostrils. She looked to the side, where Adelyn stood, as the doors clanged closed behind them.

"What did I say? That took twenty-nine minutes and thirty-seven seconds, on the nose." Adelyn sniffed with pride. "Our friend the good detective will not be bothering you, not anymore. That is, as long as you lay low for the next few days. Maybe even weeks. Do not give him further cause to stick to you like stink to shit. In due time, he'll forget all about you." She turned her attention back to her phone as it chirped. Her eyes glued to the screen, her thumb dancing over the keys.

Carly shifted from foot to foot, wondering if she should just leave as the silence drew on. "And, uh, what about what I am supposed to do?" Wanting nothing more than to put as much distance between her and the precinct as she could, she waited for an answer, or any sort of acknowledgement really, from the lawyer. Her entire body itched to get moving.

"We'll be in touch. Most likely within a few days. What you need to do for us is safe enough. You will not be engaging in any activities that'll land you on any radars that you need to worry about, not while the good detective might yet be watching." The lawyer's phone dinged no less than a dozen times as she continued to look at it, before lifting her gaze back to Carly. "Even so, we're playing it nice and slow for the time being. Don't fret, Arlene. You're in good hands with my employer. My car's here. Stay out of trouble." Before Carly could respond, Adelyn knocked on the roof of the slick, sleek black car that rolled up to the curb before ducking into the backseat.

As the door closed, Carly stared at the tinted windows, trying to catch a glimpse of the interior, of who else sat in the car before it sped off. She withdrew her phone and powered it on, waiting for it to boot up fully. Never had a loading screen taken what felt like a lifetime. She swallowed as the phone came to life.

One ding, a text.

Call me.

She sighed as her finger hovered over the *call* button. Biting her lip, looking back over her shoulder, she strode away from the precinct as quickly as she could without drawing any undue attention. *Nothing to see here*, she repeated in her mind, a mantra to ward off unwanted, if not unwarranted, attention. She imagined the weight of countless eyes watching her every step pressed against her, though that lessened with every step she put between herself and the station.

Carly looked at the unanswered text, sighed, thumbing the button as she lifted the phone to her ear. Her service must've been sluggish because her phone rang instead with someone calling her, nearly making her drop it. Her teeth worried against her lower lip as she chewed, despite knowing how much it'd hurt later. She ducked into crowds, losing herself in them.

She swallowed before speaking. "Hi, sorry, I was—"

The voice on the phone radiated with anger, and a lot of it. "Where the hell have you—"

"Listen. I got nicked for something. A camera caught me on one of the last jobs, somehow must've still been recording. I don't know how.

A detective brought me in for questioning. I didn't say anything," she whispered, taking random turns as she walked and talked. *Just in case,* she told herself.

"Shit. Shit. That's not good. Really not good." The voice on the other side paused, but Carly heard the tell-tale signs of her pacing. "Do you need me to bail you out?"

"...No, see, that's the thing. I'm free. I'm on my way home right now." She swallowed hard as silence filled the line. Only the crackle of a momentary lapse in cell reception let her know the call remained connected.

"How?" A pause, followed by a heavy sigh. "What did you do?" The voice on the other end sounded calm.

Carly knew better. *This is before the storm.*

"I didn't have a choice," she snapped before sighing as well. "Backed into a corner, I did what I had to to make sure I'm good. That we're good. I had a lawyer, an honest-to-goodness lawyer, and she danced circles around the detective."

"What did you do?"

"Sounds like someone's had an eye on us for some time. They knew." Carly looked over her shoulder, looking for any familiar faces in the crowd. Not sure which faces, or who might be following her but still, she checked. *Just in case.*

"Pray tell, what exactly did they think they know, Carly?"

She didn't answer the question and let silence build up once more. She thought she heard fingers drumming against wood. She swallowed hard and ducked into the mouth of an alleyway. Peeked back out around the corner, looking again for anyone who might be paying her too much attention. Maybe Detective Stedman.

"They know about us. *All* of us," Carly hissed.

"Who, the detective? Impossible."

"No, the lawyer. Her employer, whoever they are." She contemplated the next words as they swam in her head. "Her boss even thinks I'm you, Arlene. How weird is that?" she whispered in the quiet of the path between buildings, her attention on the long stretch of dank concrete, a dark tunnel with light at the end where it emptied out on another street. The world wobbled as she lost herself in the childhood wonder that this pathway between buildings opened a portal to somewhere else.

Somewhere better.

Arlene's voice drew her back from that fanciful ledge. "What?" The incredulity in her voice almost made Carly chuckle.

"They think I'm you. They think I'm the one, uh, in charge." *It felt nice.* She swallowed those words as laughter flooded the line.

"Oh, oh shit. That's just rich. *You?*" Arlene's laugh made Carly smile, if only through the pain. "Well, that just goes to show that you're the brightest of the bunch, at least. Which lets me dwell and lurk in the darkness, screaming unto the void." A pause, one that made Carly wince. "Did they say what they wanted? In exchange for their help?"

"Whoever it is provided me with a lawyer; Ms. Nitz. She talked circles around the detective, turning his evidence for me into circumstantial at best. Made him think twice about actually booking me today. Threatened him with harassment charges, and he backed right down. She alluded that this isn't his first rodeo with pushing bogus charges."

"Did this *lawyer* say what she wanted? Or what her employer actually wants with us? With *you.*" Arlene spoke in that tone again, making Carly wince.

"Just that her employer has taken an interest. In us, and what I can do. For them." She waited for a laugh, something, anything. "All I know is that we're supposed to become handlers. Didn't give much more than that, other than we'll be contacted soon." Checking the street one more time, the sensation of being watched still itching down her spine. "Sounded like we'd be well compensated, too. No more chump change."

"I don't like this. Not one bit. Did they give you any actual information on what we're supposed to do for them?" The energy in Arlene's voice spoke to her building dread, a feeling Carly mirrored. A job to do, but money to boot.

"There'll be a courier with a dossier within a few days and instructions. Arlene, I-I'm sorry."

"We can talk about that later. I'm not happy, but we'll make do with what we've been dealt. We can talk more when you get home, nice and quiet like. I want every detail." She paused on the phone, and Carly could just picture the calculating look on her face. "I'll contact the rest, and we'll have dinner. A family meeting. It's been some time since last we gathered proper anyway." She hung up before Carly could reply.

Nodding, if only to herself, Carly pocketed her phone. Turning away from the promise, dark though it may be, of the alley that might lead her away from everything, to disappear into the heart of the city, she returned to the street to head home.

Arlene latched onto her the moment she arrived home, unwilling to wait for more details.

Carly barely had a chance to remove her jacket before she walked Arlene through the entire ordeal, from start to end, and then again from the top. Pausing, asking questions, making Carly repeat herself, making her close her eyes, pulling out all of the tricks in the book to help her remember every detail, no matter how inconsequential.

This repeated itself over the next few days, with Carly answering every question, every time Arlene asked it. The two of them acted it out, replayed through the interrogation and the interview time and time again. Focusing on the lawyer, Adelyn, her mannerisms, and whether or not Arlene could glean any more morsels of information. Especially after Googling the lawyer turned up very little information at all.

A new fear crept into Carly as she lay down to sleep and closed her eyes, finding herself back in that room. It took everything she had to remain calm, to breathe and banish the burned-in scene of the interrogation room that haunted her every waking moment, now seeking to creep into the realm of her dreams.

A reprieve from the entire ordeal came after a few days. A loud pounding rattled the brownstone's front door enough that Carly damn near jumped out of her skin. Heart racing, breath catching in her throat, fearing the absolute worst, she stalked toward the door. Stayed away from any of the windows near the front of the house. She paused as she heard the door open, then close. She exhaled a shuddering breath.

A few moments later, Arlene walked into the dining room, carrying a sealed package.

Sitting at the table, she beckoned Carly over as she set the package down. Without waiting, she worked her fingers into and under the tape sealing it closed, unwrapping the unassuming brown paper.

Carly sat, dutifully so, waiting as Arlene methodically opened the delivery. *This must be the dossiers.* As if to answer her, her sister freed a series of envelopes from within, spreading them out over the table.

Leaning over, nervous energy making her foot tap against the floor, Carly snatched one of the manila folders. *Sabrina Hall*, a name neatly scribed across the top. No other marks or anything, just a seal binding even the dossier closed. Sliding her finger through the seal, she withdrew it and skimmed the first page. She whistled.

The noise drew Arlene's attention away from her own perusal. "What? What is it? What do you have?" She ignored her own dossier in favor of Carly's, leaning over, trying to steal a glance.

"This one, I'm not sure about the rest, but this one? She's like us." She flipped through the pages, looking at the plethora of information, trying to consume it all with a quick skim.

"What do you mean—"

Carly shot her a look. "Not like that. Not like us, *like us*. Like me. Like you. She can do things. Looks like she can manipulate time. Or look at the threads of fate, or into the past? Not a lot of details, other than she can manage short hops, but shows more potential with practice." A shiver ran through her at the thought of that power, and what it might do. She looked at the collection of files again, wondering exactly what she'd gotten them into. "What does yours say?"

"Huh. This one's just named M." Arlene held it up to show her before she worked through the seal. Once she was through, and thumbing through the pages, it wasn't long before she whistled. "Shapeshifter. Unknown the extent but can fool most basic biometric security checks. Nice." Her eyes moved over the information, her fingers drumming against the back of the folder. She shifted through a few more folders, cracking seals, skimming, sorting them out.

"What do you think?" Carly asked, somewhat hopeful. The look Arlene shot her, though, with slightly narrowed eyes, made her heart sink. "I'm sorry." Uncertain of what she apologized for—whether it was getting caught, or getting them conscripted. Maybe both.

Arlene shook her head slightly before turning her attention back to the files. "Never mind that. Call everyone in. Tomorrow night, if they can. Tell them it's an emergency." She scowled at Carly. "We'll order food in. Chinese and pizza. I'm going to go over these in the study to sort through and plan. See if I can work your blunder in this to our advantage." She took the dossier on Sabrina out of Carly's hand before she turned and strode toward the study. The door slid closed with a click of finality.

Digging through the closet, removing dusty boxes and totes full of holiday decorations and tchotchkes that hadn't seen the light of day for some time, Carly tried to find where they'd shoved the leaves for the table. With everyone being called in, they needed more room.

Once she finally unearthed them and sealed the holiday décor away for another day, she returned to the dining room to prepare the table. Extending it, so there would be plenty of room for everyone, and the copious amounts of food already ordered. No one would have cause to complain, not if she could help it. And she would.

Today has to go off smoothly. Has to. Carly repeated that over and over in her head as she cleaned the house, dusting, wiping, scrubbing, rearranging the table. Anything to burn through the nervous, anxious energy that threatened to combust inside her with Arlene's continued silence and scarcity around the house.

The house seemed to loom with quiet, because she knew that when everyone arrived, it would become confining and chaotic.

A few times, she thought to knock on the door to Arlene's study. A place Carly rarely stepped foot into, if ever. A mystery within their own house. She caught herself, fist raised to rap knuckles against the solid wood, but she stopped herself. Forced herself to ignore the turmoil eating at her from the inside, the anxiety that grew with every passing hour.

"Just nerves, right?" she spoke to herself, adjusting and readjusting the dining chairs. They were in the right place, and she had even laid out placards decorated with everyone's names. *Just in case*, she told herself. Seven seats in all, only one seat sat unclaimed, that at the head of the long table. Two chairs on one side, three on the other, and Carly claimed the one across from the head. She left the dining room and resumed fretting through the house, making sure everything else was in order.

She passed the majority of the day checking, double-checking, and even triple-checking the order for each restaurant, ensuring nothing was out of stock, or an order canceled. She reviewed the orders, again, making sure she remembered everyone's favorites, after all this time. Pizza, garlic knots, a few orders of General Tso's chicken, a pile of crab rangoon, and a dozen pork egg rolls. A cannoli for herself, and two tiramisus for Arlene.

Carly paused in her umpteenth circuit through the house, and before she could check her phone clock, or to scroll through the orders, her email, an empty inbox of texts, *something, anything* to pass the crawl of time, the brownstone's door opened. Loud sounds from the outside world filtered in, the distant din of the city. More than that, though, voices. Familiar voices outside, a conversation she could barely hear.

"Arlene, they're here," she called out, racing toward the door just in time to see an argument. *Just like old times.* "Marlie. Darlie. Charlie. Tarly." Pausing, narrowing her eyes, counting again in her head. "Where's Farlie? Never mind, I'm sure she'll show up eventually. Please, come on in. We've been waiting." Looking at herself four times over disoriented her. She ushered them inside and collected their jackets as they disappeared inside.

After Carly put everything away, she went to the dining room, where she found the kaleidoscope of her reflections all sitting at the table. Sure, they all had slightly different haircuts, and varied ways of dressing, but they were mirror images of one another. Of Carly herself. Of Arlene. They talked over each other, catching up as if it hadn't been, what? Weeks? Months? Maybe even a year since the last time Arlene had called them all back.

A *family* dinner, so to speak.

Carly caught a bottle of wine as it made its rounds, pouring herself a glass before handing it off once more. Thankfully, she'd set out a few bottles. She sipped at her glass and basked in the chatter, filling the house once more to the brim.

"Guys, okay. Almost everyone's here. Marlie, slow down on the wine. At least savor the taste," she chided, unable to help a chuckle escaping. "Seriously, though, has anyone heard from Farlie?"

"Don't worry about Farlie. I spoke to her late last night; she's taking care of her part of this business already." Arlene appeared at her side, relieving her of her wine goblet. "Here, let me hold your wine for a moment."

She looked sidelong at her sister, who appraised everyone as they ate.

"Do me a favor. Go get another bottle of wine or three from the cellar."

"Oh, I already did that. I brought them up earlier." Carly looked at the table and the seven around it once more, avoiding the look Arlene shot her. Blinking, uncertain, she nodded. "Okay, I'll go get one more. Just in case." She did just that, ducking out of the dining room toward the kitchen, and down into the cellar.

The stairs creaked beneath her feet as she padded down them as quick as she dared. The basement darkness never failed to drive a spike of fear into her, and tonight just seemed that much worse. The furnace kicked on, a grumbling growl and a rush of air whistling through the ducts, making Carly jump. Calming herself, she made quick work of grabbing another bottle and running right back up the stairs. Just in time for the doorbell to ring.

Setting the wine down on a console, Carly hurried to the door where the two delivery drivers, arms chock full of food, vied for position on the stoop. She gave them each their tip and ferried the food into the dining room, laying everything out.

Arlene sat at the head of the table, swirling Carly's wine glass in her hand.

Carly wormed her way around the table, reacquainting herself with her goblet as she passed her sister, and headed for the other end. "Marlie. That's my seat." She shook her head, motioning with her wine. "You're over there. Next to Darlie."

"I don't see why you get the head of the table," Marlie sniffed, taking one of the bottles of wine, leaving her glass behind. She carted it off as she moved over to her seat. Popping one boot up on the table as she yanked the cork out with her teeth, leaning back in her chair, taking a long swig, glaring at her all the while.

"Please take your boot off the table. Don't lean back in the chair." Carly just shook her head and sat down, cradling her glass in her hands. She swirled it, her eyes moving across her own face, cast back at her from four different bodies. Five, including Arlene. Carly snuck a glance toward her, at the other end of the table, that knowing look piercing her through and through. She gulped down another mouthful of wine, grimacing at the fluttering in her stomach.

"Why are we here?" Marlie piped up again, louder than the rest, and after a well-placed glare from Arlene, she took her boot off of the table and sat the chair back down. "Seriously, though, what's the big hubbub that we all had to come back for?" She ignored the next glare Arlene shot her, drawing another pull from her wine bottle, as if it were her lifeline.

Carly sighed, biting her lower lip as she looked at Marlie, the outlier. She almost felt sorry for her. She laughed as she realized the lie, one she often told herself. Of course she cared. Too much, sometimes. *Oh, Marlie.*

"You are not to drink all of my"—Arlene looked at Carly, grimacing again—"our wine, to start with. Slow down, sister." The growl in her voice took Carly by surprise as she gestured to her. "It seems our sister here has landed herself in a spot of hot water. Which, in turn, has ended with us all in there alongside her."

Everyone else who'd busied themselves with doling out pizza or Chinese food, sometimes both, paused.

Carly shrunk into her chair as their gazes swiveled almost as one toward her. She drained the rest of her wine and sat up a little straighter as she cleared her throat. "It's not like that. It's not *just me*. They had pictures of all—" Carly tried to speak around the lump in her throat, but Arlene waved her off. She closed her mouth, her hand moving to her throat as a cough built up.

"No, but if Detective Stedman hadn't found a trace of us in the system, and photos of you at your last assignment, we might not be in this boat. Beholden to, as of yet, a nameless and faceless player. Maybe a benefactor, maybe not. Whoever they are, they know both who and what I am. *We* are." Arlene stared at her even as she commanded attention with her presence, enough to shut the rest of them up.

Silence settled like a mantle around the room.

Carly hiccupped, heat rushing to her face. Wanting to be some-where—anywhere—else, she coughed again to clear the growing itch in her throat, squirming in her chair. *Drinking the wine on an empty stomach. Rookie move, Carly.* Her head spinning, she placed her hand on the table as if to steady the room. The walls moved closer, the floor, further away. She screwed her eyes shut as her stomach roiled, rebelled.

"As it is, we've been...conscripted," Arlene continued.

"What's that even mean? *Conscripted?*" Marlie barked, laughing. "What are we, a bottle of pills?"

"That's prescription, you fucking airhead. I swear." Arlene sighed, setting her glass down. "No, we now find ourselves in debt. And to clear that, we have been given a job. Each of us has an assignment from here on out. We'll each be watching a person with power. To start with. As needed, we will make contact and insert ourselves into their lives, so that we can learn about them. Befriend them.

"In due time, we'll pass along assignments. We'll each have our part to play in this. There's nine of them. I've already started plotting out who gets which two." Arlene lifted her glass again, taking another sip.

"Farlie's out. That leaves six of us. Who's getting stuck with more work?" Marlie mimicked Arlene by taking a long pull from the bottle of wine once more.

Carly blinked and coughed. The act of it wracked her body, and she couldn't stop. Couldn't breathe in the air that rushed out of her. She wiped her face with blood-speckled hands as she coughed again. She tried to stand, but the room spun again. Violently.

No. She looked up at the ceiling. The room itself seemed so very distant, and the last thing she saw was her own face, staring down at her. Repeated over and over again as her sisters crowded in.

"Carly's sacrificing for the rest of us. As the first of you, she's outlived her usefulness." Arlene gave each of the others a pointed look. "This is the price of failing me." Her words filtered in from so far away.

Carly tried to sit up. Tried to speak, to say something, anything. *Help.*

Someone screamed. Marlie pushed up and off the table, stood over Carly, toe-to-toe with Arlene.

"What the fuck gives you the right? Call 911. Call an ambulance. One of you get the fuck up and move. Help me! Help her!" Marlie knelt, her face hovering somewhere above her, her red hair a backlit halo. Green eyes welled with tears, and Carly tried to reach a shaking hand to brush them away.

Don't cry, Marlie. It'll be alright. But words failed her.

"She has well outlived her usefulness. Let this serve as a lesson to each and every one of you. Do not fuck up. Not again. You. Are. Expendable. And *replaceable.*" Arlene yanked Marlie to her feet and continued, "We'll have a new Carly tomorrow. Now, if you're ready to listen, we have work to get to."

The conversation dribbled off to a low, murmuring wave of words.

Carly couldn't make them out, not through the haze of pain. She tried to say something, anything. Her throat constricted against the words as the world itself dimmed. And yet, she could still hear Arlene prattling on. One by one, the faces looking over her, faces just like her own, disappeared. Leaving her alone, curled up on the floor.

Memories of her and Arlene, as children, twin sisters. Of Arlene always taking charge, leading, the first born, and never letting Carly forget it.

And then, the other sisters, created when they were older. All of those wracked her mind as whatever Arlene slipped into her wine ravaged her body. *Just like our parents.* Carly would've laughed if she could have. Even that, here, had been denied to her. Tears, or blood, or both, ran down her face as she closed her eyes.

Even now, she tried to work up the will against her failing body to say the words that had become her mantra, *I'm sorry,* but never could before the darkness took her completely.

Turn the Other Cheek

An incessant, irritating snapping of fingers drew Thorn out of his reverie, away from the half-remembered dream that faded as the world grew clearer around him. The noise drew his attention to Farlie. He blinked a few times, shoving away the remnants of a poorly timed catnap.

As she realized she had his attention, she waggled her fingers.

Am I supposed to know those hand signals? Either she wanted him to take his headphones out, or she had reconsidered his idea of ordering some tacos from somewhere nearby.

Staring at her a little longer before she rolled her eyes and pantomimed again as if he'd understand it any better, Thorn turned away from her, staring out at the window as the car circled the same city blocks for what had to be the fourth or fifth time. His gaze remained cemented to the window, the world outside, as he shifted his seat within the backseat of the giant SUV.

"Take off the headphones, Thorn," Farlie shouted from the passenger seat as she twisted in her seat, looking at him.

Half tempted to lose himself in the music by turning it louder, Thorn sighed and slid the buds out of his ears and back into their case. The sound within the van, of the surrounding traffic, roared back in and he grimaced. His hand fell to the seatbelt next to him, pulling it out, letting the rough fabric glide against his fingers as it retracted when he let go.

Farlie's radio crackled to life on her shoulder. She raised her hand, and Thorn clenched his jaw.

"Jasper is ready."

"Felix is in position."

"Sabrina is standing by."

Three voices spoke nearly over one another as they reported in, Farlie's radio loud enough that it filled the SUV. "Check, check, check. Check for Thorn as well. Sleepyhead's awake," she replied before letting her radio fall silent once more. "You *are* ready for this, right?" The side-eye she leveled at Thorn made him squirm, her vivid green eyes searching, layer by layer, digging deep.

"What's not to be ready for? I'm an insurance policy. That's it. That's what we agreed on. You said I might not even see action." Thorn crossed his arms over his chest, shaking his head. Knowing her capacity to be stubborn well outweighed his, Thorn sighed. "But should you need me, yes, I'm ready."

"Once more, with gusto, check-check for Thorn. We are go. I repeat, we are go. Proceed, nice and quiet like." Farlie had that look to her face, an almost bloodthirsty quality to it. No wonder, with enough firepower strapped to her, she looked like a modern war goddess ready to stride into battle. And yet, if everything went to plan, she'd never even get close to the eye of the storm, and neither would he. That suited him just fine.

Thorn leaned his head against the near-opaque window of the SUV, looking out at the city. Not that he could see much, for all the buildings in the way. Or the people hurrying or milling about. Twisting his neck, he looked at everyone, and then up at the sky. "Looks like there's a storm brewing."

"C'mon, dude. What's got you spooked?" Farlie asked, half a laugh in her words.

Thorn looked back at her, a sinking feeling encompassing his heart as it slammed into his stomach. "There are people. Too many. You told me the area would be mostly clear."

"Well, yeah. We had a plan for a lovely storm to be here already but, as it turns out, that simply wasn't in the cards. We'll have to make do."

She tried to play it off, but he could read her anxiety in the way her eyes flicked to the side as she lied to him. Too many nights spent playing poker with her.

"But?" he pressed, prickling sensations running along his spine.

"We had to have Jasper for today." She turned away in her seat. "Enid made sure that would happen, which threw that particular part of the plan right into the trash. She called in Nikhail, paid the price to have her brother healthy. Funny part of it is, he's so gung-ho to be part of this, he refused her when she asked him to bow out. Said it had to be him." She laughed then, a barking sound as she shook her head. "She paid the price, poor girl."

"Wait—Enid died?!"

"What? No. No, what gives you that idea?" Farlie blinked, confusion evident on her face.

"You said she paid the price. I can only imagine the cost of fixing Jasper up."

"No, no, not like that. The price to fix Jasper's powers, well, looks like it was her own." Farlie grimaced. "Trading away all of that, that's, well, huge. Stupid, but huge."

"Oof." Thorn winced, and for half a moment, considered it. Trading away one's powers to heal a loved one. For the span of maybe five heartbeats, he wondered what it would be like.

To be free of his power. *Could I make the same trade? Would I?*

If only he had someone he cared enough to try for.

"That said, everyone's checked in." Farlie placed her hand on her radio again, a smirk on her face. "This will help clear the streets, too." Pressing the button down, the radio crackled to life once more. "We are a go for operation Blind Eye. I repeat: Blind Eye is a go. Fire in three minutes."

"Roger." This time, multiple voices answered at the same time, a symphony of sameness.

Farlie tapped the masked driver on the shoulder, and he pulled into the next entrance, straight into a parking garage.

Instead of going up, the driver turned to the lower ramp and descended. Down, deeper into the belly of the earth, the bowels of the city. Concrete swallowed up the sun, until sickly, yellow lights reflecting off of the windshields of cars, painful to look at, dimly illuminated this world.

Thorn closed his eyes, waiting for the car to stop. Every passing moment drove anxiety and fear through him. One finger traced the stitching of the seat, finding where one thread frayed and stuck out from the others.

The driver parked the car, and Farlie got out. She knocked on the rear window, opening the door for Thorn.

"Why are we down here?" He slid out of the car, stretching as he went, willing muscles that screamed from being cooped up too long in the car, twisted in the wrong position from his nap, to relax. The vest she had him in ached with its weight, heavy on his shoulders. "This thing is pointless," he grunted as he futzed with the straps.

Farlie batted his hands away and took over, checking and adjusting. She made sure everything was in place. This close, standing near her, she looked up at him.

A wave of dizziness spread through him, as if he might drown in those green eyes.

"It's *my* insurance policy. Just in case," Farlie grunted as she checked and double-checked everything was right where it was supposed to be. "I know you'd rather be anywhere else, but with the way things have played out, we need you." She paused, a knowing look in her eyes, a grin plastered across her lips. "*I* need you."

Breathless, her words made his heart stutter in his chest. "You owe me for this," Thorn groused. "This thing is really uncomfortable."

"Only if things go south, and they very well might not. Until then, this is just us out for a day trip, and I owe you nothing," Farlie replied, patting his cheek as she smirked again. "Let's go."

Thorn trailed after her as she turned left, making way for the stairs up. "I want Taco Bell if this pans out, or rather, doesn't. And you're buying."

"There's no way in hell that *I* am going to buy *you* Taco Bell. Nuh uh, no way, dude."

"Fine." Thorn laughed a little as he followed her into the stairwell. "Why'd we park so far down, anyway?"

"You'll see." Farlie shot him a knowing look. Her phone beeped and, as if on cue, the lights in the stairwell went out. A moment passed before emergency ones flickered back on. These barely provided enough light to see by.

"What the fuck?" Thorn blinked in the near darkness. His hand slid into one of the straps of his vest, hooking his fingers against the edge, letting the rough fabric dig in.

"That's part one. Hurry and move that skinny ass. We do *not* want to be late to our checkpoint." Farlie didn't wait for him before she started booking it up the stairwell, boots clanging as she went.

Thorn followed suit. A part of him wanted nothing more than to run away, to get out of there. The rest of him knew that option was no longer available. This made it so that every step felt like someone else took it, someone else piloted his body and he sat in the backseat, helpless but to watch, wanting nothing more than to retreat back down. Hide from what lay on the horizon.

By the time they reached the street-level entrance, the sunlight-dappled day hurt to squint at. Which is what Thorn did as he looked out the glass doors to a city suffering cardiac arrest. The streets, the arteries of its beating heart, sat clogged with cars unmoving, engines not purring along. No radios blaring, no glaring lights on billboards.

Nothing but confused looks and conversations.

"What happened? What is this? What is going on?" He swallowed more questions, following Farlie out onto the street full of cars. That, in and of itself, looked normal at first glance.

Everyone standing outside of their cars, the lack of noise, the lack of sound, was not. People held their phones up, looking for a signal, as if that might help.

"Blind Eye is a go." A new voice, similar to Farlie's and the rest, and yet somehow different, sprung up on the radio. "Everyone, converge on the target."

"You got it, A. We're moving in and will wait at the assigned location." Farlie muted the responses from others as the sudden noise drew attention their way. Ignoring the looks from the civilians, she grabbed Thorn by the arm, dragging him along.

"You didn't answer me, Farlie." Thorn followed, shaking his arm free but not breaking stride to keep up with her.

It was only when they were clear of the rubbernecking people that she slowed enough to speak. "We took out the power to this area. A few blocks, radiating from this tower. Remi helped with that, before he bailed." She pointed to the building as she drew to a stop, holding her arm out to arrest Thorn's own forward momentum. "We wait here."

Thorn whistled at the scope of what he found himself embroiled in. "Putting a lot of eggs in this basket. I think I forgot something in the car. I'm going to—"

"Fuck you are. You're going to stay right there," Farlie growled. "We needed to isolate this building. It has its own redundant power source, but everything else around is now dark. The streets are full of dead cars, so once the alarms go off, we have ample time to do what we came for before any police response is near enough to cause worry." She withdrew a small wire-mesh box and opened it, taking out two earpieces. She handed one to Thorn. "Here."

He took the device and slid it into his ear. It came to life on its own, a low thrum inside his head that slowly became voices. Other voices that sounded almost just like Farlie's. His head spun trying to make sense of how he heard so many copies of her when she stood silent next to him. His heart raced, adrenaline spiking.

"Is everyone ready to go?" Farlie this time, her voice clear in both his ears.

Thorn's head spun as he tried to ignore the nagging feeling that crept along his spine. *Shit. Shit. I shouldn't be here. Why did I agree to this?* He curled his hands into fists around the straps of his vest, the fabric and Velcro digging into his skin. The pain helped—if only a little—calm him down so that he could focus. On her, on the conversations.

"Jasper, you're up." An echo of Farlie over the wire, followed by silence.

"Let's get this show on the road." That must've been Jasper. Thorn couldn't help but wince at the cocksureness of that voice, wishing he felt half the same level of confidence. "I have the passcodes. The latest patrol passed by two minutes ago. I'm going in three...two...one."

Thorn winced against an audible popping noise followed by horrendous feedback.

"Darlie, check in. What was that?" Farlie growled out the words.

"Check. Check." A pause. "We're in. I think he fried his radio on the way. I'm still here, though. Hey, Jasper, check your nose." A rustling noise filled the line before Darlie spoke again. "It's empty in here. Huh."

Another pause that went on entirely too long.

"Fuck."

A sharp spike of static and feedback pierced the connection before silence returned. Thorn winced at the aftershock of the loud noise and counted every second by the thrum of his heartbeats, waiting for the connection to reestablish.

Farlie fidgeted from foot to foot, her nervousness infectious.

Thorn swallowed hard.

"I don't like that." Her voice came only to him and not through the earpiece. She tapped at her own ear, to no avail. Her curses were enough to almost make Thorn blush with their vehemence. "Let's move in closer."

Before he could answer, she moved.

Not willing to be left behind, or alone, Thorn bustled after her, near running to catch up. He met and matched her stride as they neared the building. With every step, the hairs on the back of his neck stood that much straighter. A shiver raged through him.

Farlie leaned this way and that in front of the doors, as if trying to see the inner workings of the building. "Tarly. Darlie. Check the fuck in right now."

"Give them a moment. They might be fine, but unable to check in," Thorn offered, but his stomach had already sunk. Something felt wrong, off. He immediately wished he could take those words back as Farlie shot him a glare, making him recoil.

"The fuck they are. We're going in." She yanked the door open, motioning him ahead.

The blandness of the lobby's design made it hard to focus on any one point, convincing a casual visitor that there was nothing to see there. Nothing stood out, nothing caught his eye, except for the distinct lack of people. As soon as the door closed behind them, the strobing light and wail of a siren filled the room, making him flinch.

The televisions behind the receptionist desk flickered to life, with a series of one unremarkable face repeated across them. That face, and its mirrors, stared at Farlie.

And Thorn.

How he knew the face stared at him, he couldn't guess. Maybe it was how the eyes darted between him and Farlie, showing an emotion that never registered on the face, which remained placid, serene. Almost too calm, just as bland as the lobby. Too perfect, maybe, and the smile that started to creep across it far too wide.

Thorn's toes curled in his boots, his stomach threatened to shrivel up, and a cold sweat broke out over his brow and nape, trickling down the back of his shirt, and the bulletproof vest.

"This isn't going to plan, is it? Are we fucked? We're fucked." His whisper sounded foreign to his own ears.

"Fucked proper, I think," Farlie whispered back, a gun in each hand as she squared off against the multitude of faces from the televisions, as if she meant to shoot them out. Maybe she would.

"What have you gotten me into?"

"Exactly what I told you. For the moment, I suggest you remember this is exactly what you agreed to do. Do not—and I will repeat this again, very slowly for you—do not fuck around on me." She checked her guns and flicked off the safeties before holstering one. "This is about to get real. Really real, and I need you focused and on point. Got it?"

"...Taco Bell," Thorn grunted as he stepped around her. Her empty hand gripped his shoulder. Thorn closed his eyes and breathed in, deep, counting to himself. *One. Two. Three.*

Across the lobby they walked, with Farlie sticking to him from behind. Nothing, except for the now-flickering creep on the screens and the room painted in the siren's light, and the warbling klaxon of warning. Thorn jabbed his finger into the call button for the elevator, half surprised it actually worked.

As if reading his mind, Farlie spoke, leaning closer as the elevator started to ding its way down to them. "Felix should be in the security console room. Keeping us with access. I hope."

Thorn pressed the button a few more times, as if that might magically speed the process up. "As much as I hate to say it because my legs are tired, maybe we should take the stairs."

"No can do, Thorn. Stairs are out of the question today. They're set up like a death trap. Funnily enough, the elevators are the only way up right now. If this is going the way we expect, Felix bypassed their armory floor and sent the elevator straight to us. They're likely scrambling to find a way around his control of the system."

He shook his head. "There's a lot of *ifs* in that spiel that makes me decidedly uncomfortable, Farlie. This elevator might open, and we might chew on a hail of bullets, too."

She squeezed his shoulder. "Have a little faith. Anyway, not if you can help it, right?"

"Listen, this is beyond the scope—"

"No. *You* listen. You're going to be *fine*. I trust you." She tightened her hand again.

Thorn swallowed hard, nodding. He didn't need to look behind him to see the smirk on her face; the reflective surface of the elevator showed it to him. The fun-house mirror effect made it that much more unnerving, her face warping and shifting.

The doors opened with a ding. For half a moment, he expected there to be people within it, staring at him, weapons drawn. Seeing, instead, that it sat empty, they stepped inside. They turned as one so that he faced the doors and she stayed behind him. In the confines of the elevator, his heart thrummed that much louder. His ears roared with the crescendo of his own adrenaline as it drowned out the soft music that played over the speaker.

"Are you ready?" Farlie asked again, leaning into him, a slight purr to her voice.

"You really do pick the oddest times to get cuddly, you know that, right?" Thorn laughed as he spoke, incredulous. "To answer you, though: I am as ready as I can be, knowing this is already fucked, and we've never run a test scenario at this potential scale."

"Have as much faith in yourself as I do, Thorn. You've got this. Trust me, trust in yourself."

"And if I don't 'got this'? What then? People are going to die." He looked at her over his shoulder. "You're going to die."

Farlie searched his face. "People are going to die anyway. That was always on the table."

"That's not the same. I don't want the others to get hurt." Thorn looked back to the number slowly climbing on the elevator's panel over the door. "Or you."

"Do what you do, and that's not going to be an issue. As for the others, they can handle themselves. Don't think about them. Worry about you. And me. That's all we need, you and me. Me and you."

The elevator started to slow.

"Here we go." Farlie leaned away from him as she crouched.

"Fuck me running." Thorn sighed, closing his eyes as his head spun, his stomach threatening to revolt.

The elevator dinged.

The doors slid open. Thorn opened his eyes. Marble flooring, gilded wood paneling, pillars.

And a slew of uniformed people, masks over their faces, all turning away from the solid double doors on the other side. Weapons moved, training on him in what might've been a lovely laser show were they not ready to let bullets fly.

"Go," Farlie commanded.

Thorn stepped out of the elevator, running a finger over the rough edge of his vest.

In answer, an echoing chorus of barked out commands and safeties being released filled the room.

"Stop!"

"Stand down!"

"Take one more step and we open fire!"

Everything tapered off into tense silence.

Thorn stepped forward again.

"That's it, open fire!"

A laser centered right on Thorn's chest, where the bullet-proof vest sat over his heart. Time dilated as he watched the bullet fly closer, closer, closer, the tip collapsing into itself as it slammed into his vest. He expected a shock of pain, a thudding kick knocking him off his feet.

That never happened.

Instead, the bullet reversed trajectory, speeding back to whence it came. Straight for the heart of the one who fired it.

Blood exploded from their chest as the bullet tore through them. Gurgling coated the stunned silence as they collapsed.

"FIRE! FIRE! FIRE!"

Like thunder came a furious flurry of gunfire, with the pitter-patter of ejected shells like raindrops, and the lightning of muzzle flashes. A hailing storm of violence, with Thorn at its eye.

Too many bullets sped through the air, and Thorn braced himself. *Fuck, fuck, fuck.* Rinsed and repeated for every bullet. He flinched from the onslaught, the pings of concrete and metal when those bullets missed. Those bullets that should've connected, though, turned on their owners.

Blood filled the air like a haze, mixing with the stench of cordite and fear.

"STOP! STOP!" Another order barked over the chaos, but one that went unheeded. The bullets continued to fly and ricochet.

Until they didn't.

Thorn blinked, looking away from the dead and dying, and looked back at Farlie. "You okay?"

"I'm as right as the mail." She bared her teeth in a vicious grin. "I knew you had it in you. Let's find the others. They should be holed-up in the control room over there." Without further preamble, she moved around him and headed for the door.

Thorn followed, daring a backward glimpse at the sheer carnage wrought against the elevator and its surroundings. Bullet holes pockmarked every surface in a caricature of his outline. Ahead, though, the floor lay painted in bloody bodies, those who caught the bullets meant for him.

Swallowing a laugh, if only to stave off the horror of the scene, he followed Farlie through the obstacle course of corpses. Gore soaked the marble, making the path treacherous. Viscous viscera squelched with every step, despite doing his best to follow in Farlie's footsteps.

Once past it all, Farlie straightened, pounding her fist against the shuttered metal doors covered with burn-marks and scratches. "Looks like they were trying to get in. We got here just in time." She rapped again, harder this time. "Open up!"

A muffled sound came from the other side and after a few moments, the door hissed loudly as it unsealed and opened. A mirror image of Farlie stood on the other side, a pistol at the ready, gripped in both hands as she leveled it.

"Darlie. You can stand down. We're safe until their backup arrives. We have a few minutes, I think." Farlie put her own gun away, with Darlie mirroring the movement. "Felix, give me a sitrep."

The man sitting at one of the desks peeked up around the computer, looking gaunt, eyes sunken. "There is a slim chance of their backup getting here quicker. Maybe. I managed to seal off most of the communications in and out of here as quickly as I could. It definitely bought us some time. Not much, but no external alarms have been triggered as far as I can tell." Felix paused. "Yet." He stared at Farlie pretty hard, an unspoken message clear on his face, even if Thorn had no idea what it meant. Felix gave the slightest shake of his head, scowling as he turned his attention back to the computer, fingers dancing over the keyboard.

"Everyone back in. Felix, seal it up." Farlie stepped into the room, and Thorn followed as the doors started closing with a quiet whir. She looked around. "Where's Jasper?"

Darlie looked away at that, toward one of the side walls of the room. Farlie looked, and Thorn followed her gaze.

She blanched. "Oh. Fuck me, that's not a pretty way to go."

Thorn had to lean around her so he could see why.

Half a person hung rigid, sticking out of the wall. Arm outstretched, straining, fingers reaching for something unseen. His face twisted in a rictus of pain, half of it swallowed, one with the wall.

Bile tickled the back of Thorn's throat. He forced himself to look away from the macabre sculpture. Between that and the field of corpses he walked through, he barely managed to avoid tossing his cookies. He forced himself to take a moment to just breathe, to calm his nerves. He busied himself with studying anything, everything else. Especially the people in it with him.

The room contained only one desk, which sat burdened with multiple monitors connected to a tower. Each screen scrolled through a nonstop feed of numbers, connection to the cameras, information he could hardly understand. Not that he could focus on it for long enough to bother trying.

The only part of the room that caught his attention was the other set of doors across from the sealed ones. One way out, to a field of death. Another, leading to who knew what, or where.

I should have asked so many more questions.

"Thorn, wake up. Pay attention." Farlie dragged his attention back. "I need you aware and on my six. Just in case." She watched him for a moment before looking at Darlie. "What the fuck happened here?"

"He miscalculated the jump getting us through. I think. I don't know what happened." Darlie shook her head, the blood draining out of her face. "I just know...oh fuck, I can still hear his screams." She shuddered, swallowing hard.

Thorn did so too, if only out of reflex as his resolve threatened to shatter.

"Hold it together, Darlie. We're almost there. We can deal with that mess later." Farlie sighed. "Where's Sabrina?"

"Here." A quiet voice came from in front of the computer desk. A haggard looking woman, wrinkles adorning her face around an old scar across her cheek, her hair more silver than black, stood, dusting herself off.

Farlie blinked. "...Sabrina? What the hell happened to you?"

"Don't ask." This, from another spitting image of Farlie who stood up as well, her hand reaching for Sabrina, as if to help steady her.

"Stop mothering me, Tarly," she growled.

Farlie narrowed her eyes slightly. "Can you still do what we need?"

Thorn knew that face. She was scared but wouldn't—dared not—show it.

Sabrina nodded. "I can give you about thirty seconds. Once. Maybe twice." A pause, before she nodded again, shoving free of Tarly and pacing around the room. "I could've saved Jasper."

Silence drawled out, everyone looking at one another, or pointedly not. Thorn licked his lips, looking sidelong at Farlie as if she might have an answer. He sidled a little closer to her, not daring to let too much distance come between them.

"Well, ho-kay then. Now that we're all here, let's rock and roll. We can begin the last phase." Farlie looked at Felix as she spoke, pointing toward the other set of doors. "I have the passcodes to unseal the inner chamber."

"What's in there, anyway?" he asked, adjusting himself in the seat in front of the computer. "What's all of this for?"

"You'll see soon enough. Bring up the chamber protocol, please." Farlie motioned again, waving her hand at the computer.

Felix, who started typing at the computer, made a face that somehow escaped her notice. Thorn noticed and bit back a laugh.

After a few moments, Felix scooted over to the side and motioned to Farlie. Thorn leaned over, trying to catch a glimpse, but Farlie wasted no time ducking closer.

Typing away at the keyboard, she paused, entered a few more strokes, and hovered her finger over the enter key. "Here we go, boys and girls. Hold on tight." With that, she slammed down.

Nothing happened. Silence.

Then chaos broke out as another alarm sounded, this one harsher for how it echoed in the confines. The lights dimmed to red. The ventilation system clicked shut, and the low rumble of the air circulator stopped, replaced by hissing as swirling vapor started to fill the room.

"*Incorrect password. Termination in progress. Have a nice day.*" A voice, unduly cheery, chimed from the computer, which promptly darkened, a bluish smoke emanating from the electronics adding to the quickly growing haze and stench of burning silicon.

"We're fucking sealed in." Felix hammered at the keyboard, now dead, as if he might resuscitate the system. "What the fuck? I thought you said you had this?" He shot a glare toward Farlie.

"I did." She hesitated. "I do. Sabrina? A little help?" She coughed out the words, barely able to get them out through the thick miasma.

Thorn struggled to breathe, tried to not, found that impossible. His throat started to close, his eyes unfocused and watering as pain radiated through every inch of his body. A cough wracked him, forcing him to take another burning lungful of air, of whatever else still pumped into the room.

"Fuck," Sabrina managed, screwing her eyes shut. Sweat dripped over her brow, the muscles on her neck corded and stuck out as she panted. "There." Blood trickled from her nose, which she quickly wiped away.

The room sat as normal as before around them, the lights bright, the siren unsounded.

"What the shitting fuck? I thought Phoebe got the passwords?" Farlie growled, slamming her hand on the desk.

"Ten passcodes, right? What are they?" Felix nudged her out of the way as he claimed the desk once more. He rummaged through the drawers until he found a writing pad and a mechanical pencil. Clicking the lead a few times before shoving it back in, and giving it one final click, he looked at her. "Go."

"Jury. News. Norm. Keep. Accident. Evaluate. Arm. Consultation. Fish. Plain." Farlie watched over his shoulder while he scribbled them down.

Felix stared at the list of words, the pencil moving through them over and over. "Sabrina, how many more attempts do we have? I have an idea. I think."

"That's it, I'm afraid. I'm burned out." She shook her head, grimacing. "Maybe one more, if I *had* to. And even then, I can't promise it'd work."

Silence descended in the room, all but for the sounds of Felix furiously writing, scratching out, and writing again across the pad of paper. Erasing, writing, scribbling, drawing lines, working with the list of ten words while Thorn and the rest watched.

After some time, Felix spoke. "There." He tossed the pencil down on the table, cracking his knuckles and his neck before scrubbing fingers through his hair.

"Are you certain?" Farlie asked. "Like, really, really certain? We're placing all of this on you. I need you to be right so I'll ask again: are you certain?"

"As certain as I can be. If these are the keys to the proverbial kingdom that we need, and we operate on the idea that Phoebe *did not* royally fuck up, and she's not known for that, then we're left with logic dictating that we're missing something." He chewed on his lip as his fingers danced in the air above the keyboard without quite touching it.

Farlie leaned closer. "What are you thinking?"

Thorn stepped closer too, converging with everyone around the computer.

"One of my field trips, back in elementary school." Felix barked out a laugh. "Fuck, that was ages ago. Anyway, we took a trip to the Cryptologic Museum, in Maryland. Small little place, but huge to me. It opened my eyes. That's where I got my start with all of this." He waved a hand at the computer, the words, as if they meant something to anyone but him.

"And? We're running out of time." This from Tarly, who fell silent as Farlie glared at her.

"A ten-word passcode seems secure, but it was wrong. So there has to be something else. One of the simplest forms of ciphering text is to shift every letter by a certain number of digits. In this instance, the true passcode might be those ten words, shifted by..." Felix paused, looking back at the pad of paper.

A hammering at the doors behind them made them all jump.

"Hurry up. Looks like backup is here," Farlie growled, reaching for her gun.

"My guess is either the pass codes are shifted by the number of words there are, or their ordinal position in the overall list. A progressive Caesar cipher." Felix cocked his head, closing his eyes. "Just the number ten is too simple. If this were me, I'd keep it easily remembered, but with a trick. A twist." His fingers returned to the keyboard as he started typing.

"Better be sure. Either someone's coming in through that door, or we're going to die here together, gasping." Farlie checked her gun. Tarly and Darlie did the same.

Thorn busied himself with checking his vest, if only for something to do. Anything, to preoccupy his mind from the fact he might be dying for the second time at any moment.

"Ordinal position it is." Felix slammed his finger on the enter key.

Thorn drew a deep breath. All of them did. In case it was their last clean one.

They waited.

Nothing happened.

Until the smaller set of doors hissed open. A wall of fog escaped from within, accompanied by a blast of cold, cold air. Cold enough to make Thorn shiver as the sweat on his skin went clammy.

Judging by everyone else's reaction, he wasn't the only one to feel the sudden blast of arctic temperature spreading throughout the room.

Thorn jumped as another thud slammed into the main entrance. Looking over his shoulder, he blinked. His brain failed to process the rather comical imprint of a fist protruding from this side of the door. Not until another thud—and another fist-shaped dent—appeared, making the metal of the larger doors groan.

"Yes! About damn time," Farlie shouted, and Thorn winced at the sound as it rebounded. She ignored the dreadful cold, though he saw a shiver run through her, as she stepped closer to the escaping clouds.

"Farlie, we, uh, we might have a problem." He gulped, another wave of cold running through his body. His bones felt brittle, the cold quickly overtaking the room's occupants. Taking a step away from the entrance as another thud, another protrusion, appeared, he grimaced.

Everyone else followed suit, putting distance between themselves and the persistent knocker on the other side.

"We have time. Everyone, form up. Over here," Farlie barked, Tarly and Darlie moving to where she pointed, collecting guns as she handed them out. They each checked their weapons, facing off against the door. Sabrina and Felix looked at one another before standing behind the three well-armed redheads. Well, two redheads and one whose roots were showing through the black.

Thorn stayed put, standing nearer the door. Farlie looked at him, a half a smirk twisting her lips ever so slightly upward as she nodded at him. Bracing himself, he took his own stand in front of the door. He inhaled deeply, filling himself, pulling as much as he could despite how the cold burned his lungs. He held it, counted to four, released.

With that air he pushed all of his anxiety and fear out of his body. Tried to find some level of calm as he breathed deeply again, held it, and repeated the process. Focusing his gaze on the door—which wobbled in its frame as another series of thuds landed against it, bowing the metal slabs inward—Thorn nodded, if only to himself.

"What now?" he asked, waiting for the moment the doors would give in to the abuse.

Farlie, Tarly, and Darlie spoke as one, three voices filling the room. "We do what we came here for; we finish the job. Together, we can handle what's on the other side of that door for as long as we need to. We cannot fail, not here, not now. Not this close to finishing what we started."

"Which is what, exactly?" Felix pointed at the room behind them, where the cold drafts flowed still, falling, burying the ground in a roiling, swirling fog.

"You will see in due time. Don't worry about it. Focus on surviving," the three responded.

"*What is in there?*" Felix growled, his voice reverberating through the walls.

Upon hearing *that* voice, the threat inherent in it, Thorn broke his attention from the door to glance at the trio. Each flinched away from the power of that voice. He grimaced, and started to step backward, before Farlie nodded toward the door. A part of him wanted to answer that question, even if he had no earthly idea of the answer. He could only watch the three identical faces as they struggled to speak, to say something, anything.

Without being able to.

Thorn finally stepped back, moving to place himself bodily between Felix and the rest. "Hey. Hey. We're on the same team, man."

"Some team." Felix rolled his eyes, his hands flailing. "You know what? Fuck you. Fuck these three, and most of all? Fuck all of this." Felix circled his hand around the room, before rubbing it over his face. "Fucking Marlie look-a-likes aren't worth the trouble. I should've fucking left town. At least M had the sense to get the hell out of Dodge when the getting was still good."

Thorn held his hand up, trying to walk Felix back from the edge evident in his steely eyes. "Listen, slow your roll. Whatever's in there, we're this close to winning. Help me hold the door. Help me help us get the fuck out of here. Alive."

"*Tell me what's in there,*" Felix growled again, his voice that much louder, the command that much harder to resist.

Thorn opened his mouth, to spill the guts he didn't have, but someone beat him to the punch.

A new voice, raspy with disuse, joined the fray.

"I am."

A Long, Cold Sleep

LOCKED IN THE COLD embrace of a sleep not-so-gently forced upon me, I still felt the threads of the world at large. My mind raced inverse to the sluggish blood that coursed through my veins. Cold. That is all I remembered, all I knew, all I was, and could ever be.

Cold.

I fucking *hate* the cold.

Time ceased to have meaning. Trapped, I could not move a muscle, no matter how much I wanted to. I could not scream, and yet the sound built in my throat.

At first, I remained trapped within the frigid, frozen shell of my own flesh, as if I were tapping away from the inside, trying to regain control, to break out into the real world once more. Whatever needle they shoved into my arm, whatever cocktail of unknown drugs accompanied the bone-numbing cold, stole everything from me. My body, my mind, all that I knew.

Except, I knew I hated the cold.

In time, I realized as trapped as my flesh kept me, I could still *feel* the world around me. It started small, a glimpse, that's the best word for it, for the tiny room serving as a tomb.

My tomb.

Before long—not that I could tell when it started—I realized I could let my mind wander further out through the darkness. To the web spread out before me, one I'd instinctively known, but now, with the waking world no longer drowning it out, I could explore it freely. A myriad of lives, of fates, of hopes and dreams, enshrouded before me. Darkness surrounded me.

Nothing but darkness and cold. Did I mention that? I probably did, it consumed most of my waking thoughts, such as they were. Unable to shiver, unable to find warmth.

That is, until I felt a vibration on the web that drew what little of my attention remained. Over time, I found more and more anomalies within the web. Nothing big, nothing earth-shattering, but...could they be enough?

Would they? They had to be.

An addict with a silver tongue.

A stage magician always hungering for the next spotlight.

His sister who always looked out for him, never mind the turmoil of her own life and emotions.

A person little more than a shadow in their own life, being everything to everyone.

Someone all too eager to leap, never looking down.

A person prone to living in their past mistakes, dwelling and unable to fix them.

A shut-in, content to watch out the window, or listen through the walls

A good soul who only wanted to help but knows everything comes with a cost.

Twins, echoing opposites of one another, who love to use that to their advantage.

And lastly, a person so afraid to let someone close enough be hurt, they lash out at everyone first.

These people, small pieces on a board I could not touch, I could not move, and yet...their threads called to me. I could, maybe... I *nudged* them. Nothing major, nothing untoward, not really. From afar, from a long, cold distance, I helped them become who they are.

What they are.

Not unlike playing the world's worst game of Jenga. By the slightest touch, unable to see, hear. Unable to do much more than...tap. And I did. I poked and prodded, until the web wove tighter about itself, plucking pieces out of my way when necessary. For the most part, I brought the pawns I needed together.

Convergence.

Into the series of contingencies in place, knowing my ultimate fate, and accepting it. That I might bide my time, in the darkness and cold, to rise like the phoenix.

More nudges, more vibrations on the web. Lives that might never have crossed paths in normal circumstances, woven together. Working from the darkness, I did so by the briefest, barest of touches, their lives sharp against my will. That is the baton I had to work with, and I'd like to consider myself a maestro.

A conductor, unable to hear or see my own symphony. I felt the spiders in my web as they crept closer and closer. Some disappeared, which I mourned if only for a moment. The rest soldiered on.

Their nearness brought me to the surface of the confines of my mind, my body, to the brim of the frozen chill that bound me. I twitched a finger even through all of that, and a more profound awareness of the world outside flooded in.

At first, I took it for a sick and twisted dream, one I had longed to lose myself in for time immemorial. What might have been days, or years, or decades ended as succinctly as that as I woke up. From a nap. From a coma that lasted a lifetime or more.

I could not tell either way, not that it mattered.

My body ached in ways I had never imagined. Pain coursed through me, counterpoint to the shiver that finally wracked my body. I opened my eyes, looking at the clouds of foggy air hissing to escape from the chamber that held me. With the cold swept away, I heard a furor just beyond my sight, echoing in the chilly air.

"Tell me what's in there."

That voice made me smile. The power, raw and simple, coiled snakelike within the words, held no sway over me.

I answered anyway.

"I am."

Hearing my own voice as if from a vast distance, raspy and painful to even speak, I struggled against the weight of the world rediscovered, weighing on me, and collapsed against the imprint my body left in the padding of the chamber. Tight, like a sarcophagus, it refused to let me go.

"It's time to wake up from a long, cold sleep. Let us help."

My eyes blurred, trying to focus on the owner of the voice. I saw triple—a lovely redhead with piercing green eyes hovering over me. And yet, no. There were three of them, even if one hid behind a fading dye job. I nodded, which took a lot more out of me than I cared to admit. Their hands found the needle in my arm, and more. Without much in the way of grace, they freed me from the chemicals keeping me bound within the cold.

"How long?" I swallowed, a dry convulsion of my throat. Itching set in as my body started to awaken.

Farlie, Darlie, and Tarly helped me sit up the rest of the way.

I looked down at my thin, gaunt body beneath white scrubs, grimacing at the cold. "Must get warm."

A haggard man who could almost match my own thinness stepped up, his finger pointing at me. "Who the fuck is this? What the hell is going on?"

"Stand down," I said with more of a growl to my voice than I intended.

"Not until I get some answers. *Who* are you? What are we doing here?" The man jabbed a finger with every word.

I took the bottle of water Farlie handed to me, took note of her hand on the butt of one of her guns. "Felix, right? Felix, my boy, I am, quite simply, the reason you exist as you are today. As something super."

A not-so-distant thundering thud, and the complaint of metal nearly pushed past its limit, drew Farlie's attention. I followed her gaze as I sipped gingerly at the water.

She reached into one of the pockets of her tactical pants and yanked out a small leather case. I winced as she opened it and withdrew yet another syringe and murky vial from within. I would have shuddered at the gauge of the needle on a good day. I nearly knocked it out of her hands as she brought it nearer to me. Along with the cold, I hate needles.

"You know this will help." Farlie clucked her tongue at me. Tarly and Darlie grabbed my arm, the looks on their faces saying they'd rather be anywhere else.

"Do it," I grunted, looking away from the trio, focusing on the warmth of four hands on my arm. I hissed at the pressure of the thick needle piercing through paper-thin flesh, followed by searing pain only amplified by the cold still permeating every piece of me.

"Hold him steady." Farlie bit her lip, her hand on the needle as she waited.

I drew a deep breath. Nodded again. I almost wished to be lost in the cold nothingness.

Farlie slammed the plunger home.

At first, nothing happened. Very quickly, that changed as fire coursed through my body, traversing my veins, spreading from my arm to the tips of my toes. The top of my head tingled, and I could have sworn I bent over backward to escape the sensation of my entire body liquefying. Freezing. Burning. Lightning might have struck too.

That was what it felt like, being brought back from the brink of death.

When I came to, I looked up at those three near identical faces, each full of concern. I waved off their hands as I tried to sit up again unassisted. When that worked without too much straining, I hoisted myself up on trembling arms that I might place weight on legs that refused to listen. And I refused to let them. Sheer determination carried me further, kept my legs from buckling until I felt steady enough. I walked out of the small chamber and into the room that tripled in size the world I had known for—

"How long?" I looked around at those gathered. I knew them, even if I had never seen their faces, not like this. Not in person. *Felix. Thorn. Sabrina. Ah.* I stepped over to the wall and cupped Jasper's cheek, patting it gently before turning away from the body sticking halfway out of the wall. *Sacrifices must be made.*

"Based on our research and intel? Ten years, thirty-seven weeks, four days. Give or take a few hours." Tarly handed me the water bottle from where it had fallen. I stared at it for a moment before draining the rest of the contents, tossing the bottle aside.

Another thud at the door, this time hard enough to put cracks in the frame, drew my attention. I stretched my back, my arms up and over my head, reaching for the ceiling even as I stepped up on the tips of my toes. I could not help but groan in relief, and release, as my muscles protested before they gave in.

"What the shit do you think you're doing now?" Felix stepped in front of me, his finger in my face.

I sighed, and bit down on the temper that threatened to rise. "I am preparing for what's on the other side of that door. Much as I suggest you do, instead of waggling that finger in my face like you plan to lose it." I cracked my neck first to the left, then to the right, before reaching to touch the ground between my feet.

Felix let out a string of curses before whirling on Farlie. "Marlie died for what? We're all going to die for this... I don't even have words. Why are we doing this?"

She started to answer, but I waved her off. "For me. You are doing this because of, and for, me. Have I not yet made that clear?"

Felix spun to face me again. "And who the fuck do you think you are, grandpa?"

I blinked, laughing. "Why, *I* am the reason you are standing here. I am the reason behind who, no, what, you are, Felix." I turned to look at

Thorn, and then Sabrina. "Both of you, as well. Jasper, too." I sighed, shaking my head. "And the rest. Though they were not needed at this juncture."

"And you led us here, to, what? Be captured in some cockamamie plan at best? Or be ground to paste when the supes yank that door open at worst?" Felix shouted, his voice echoing in the room.

I did not answer him, not immediately. Neither did anyone else. I let the quiet of the room be reply enough for the moment. I walked up to the door, battered and dented with the shape of a fist larger than my own head. I placed my hand over one of the indentations and grinned. I turned away from it and paced, if only to stretch my legs a little more.

"Why are you smirking? Just, *who the fuck are you?*" Felix demanded. Or tried to. Whether he failed to catch on, or simply did not care that the power in his voice could not touch me, I could not tell. The anger in him, though? That spoke to me. That language I very much understood.

"I am Weaver." I did not bother to look at the rest of them as I spoke. The near-collective gasp told me all I needed to know. They knew my name.

Good.

"*The* Weaver?"

"The one and only." I nodded and stopped in the middle of the room. I turned all of my attention on the door that fell silent a moment before.

No more thuds. No more dents or screams of metal.

Silence.

I wondered who stood on the other side, and if the silence meant they knew. That I stood, once more, a free man.

"Oh shit, oh damn, oh. Oh. Oh," Thorn stammered, stepping away quickly, as if to find somewhere to run away to, nearly tripping over his own feet in the process. Not that there was anywhere else to go but through the doors I stood in front of.

Farlie, Tarly, and Darlie looked at one another, then back at me before arming themselves once again, moving to stand behind me. I nodded to them.

Felix placed himself in my path again, between me and the only doorway out of this tiny room. While the size of it was gigantic in comparison to the small coffin of glass and metal that trapped me for so long, I knew it could not hold me. Not for much longer. Oh, how I longed to break out of this room.

Felix crossed his arms over his chest. "Why should we help you?"

"Why? There are two parts to that question. As I stated, you are who and what you are, you can *do* what you *do* because I willed it. Each and every one of you is here at my behest. And at my pleasure. As to the other part, the real why of it is because I am your only way out of this room alive. Free.

"Please take note of the quiet we find ourselves in. Observe that the door remains closed when they were so near breaking in. They know, by now, that you did not trip the safety protocols, that you are not gasping your last dying breaths. They have since surmised that you managed to open my cage, free me, and counteract the reagents they had flooding my system."

"Which means what, exactly?" Felix blinked as he spoke, looking back at the door that held my attention so raptly.

"They know I am free. And they are scared. As they should be. Which means you have a choice, here and now. Join me. Walk through those doors with me—"

"Or?" Thorn, moving to stand next to Felix, interjected even though he spoke with decidedly less confidence.

"Or..." I trailed off, taking another step.

Felix, to his credit, stood his ground. Thorn shied a step back, closer to the door.

"I'll leave you to figure that out for yourself. I could not care less about you once I step outside those doors if you stand back. I might mourn you later if you choose poorly. But for now: join me or get out of my way." I looked at those gathered, knowing a few of my pieces had wandered off. Errant children, to be brought back to the fold. No one can escape my web once caught. *M, I know you're out there.*

"I'm in." Thorn puffed up with bravado as he answered, but I saw the varying shades of fear lurking behind his eyes.

Felix nodded. "Put like that, I'm in too."

The two stepped out of the way enough that I could pass, falling in behind me as I did so.

"Us, three," Farlie, Tarly, and Darlie chimed in as one, flanking me with the two men.

"I'm, uh, I'm not actually sure I can be of any use." Sabrina, quiet, in the corner.

I beckoned her closer.

She hesitated at first, looking from me to the room around us, as if she might divine another way free. Another way out. Or if she'd dare risk using her power or die trying. Seeing no help, nowhere to run, she stepped closer.

"You would not be here, were that the case." I cupped her cheek, turning her head, dragging her eyes to mine. "I know what you have been through. I wish it could have been some other way."

She started to open her mouth, to say something, but ended up biting her lip.

"I know there are questions, I know each of you has them, and in due time, I will answer them. For now, though, we have a door, and what lies beyond, to deal with." I closed my eyes, and breathed in, filling my lungs with warm air. By the time I opened them once more, withdrawing my hand from Sabrina, most of the gray had faded from her hair. That scar on her cheek remained, though.

"I cannot take it all, but I will take some of your burden," I whispered, quiet enough for her to hear. The look in her eyes let me know she'd be on my side for life.

Good.

"Shall we?" I stepped up to the door and placed a hand on it. I felt every little piece of it, down to each molecule, and twisted them, rearranged them, bent them to my will. The door bent out of shape, ripping and tearing like the paper that suddenly comprised it. Shredded paper flew every which way, and I stepped through it.

A glaring rotation of red lights and alarm bells flooded the room as the tattered remnants of the door gave way to the lobby beyond, littered with corpses and cordite. Shouts filled the room as superheroes scrambled for cover behind the pillars.

"Weaver is free!"

"Oh fuck, call for backup! Call for backup!"

"Are you kidding? We *are* the backup! FUCK!"

"FIRE!"

Spreading my arms, I waited for the onslaught to come. Even if I did not recognize the superheroes standing guard over the freedom I so craved, I knew what powers they planned to send against me.

First, the hero in the lead, who boldly leapt at me and died almost as quickly.

All of the strength in the world, skin like titanium, none of that mattered. Not against the strobing red light of the alarms that I called to me, wrapping the beams around my fingers, drawing them taught. A crisscrossed lattice work of thin light, focused and hardened into a heat well beyond searing.

Moving my fingers in a pattern, drawing them together, apart, around one another with precise movements, I spun the light about our intrepid hero and *pulled*.

I yanked harder against what little resistance his super skin provided, with muscle and sinew sloughing apart next. Light moved to my whim and will, and I drank in the fear I saw in the hero's eyes before he fell to pieces.

"This is the point where maybe you should run for help." I spread my hands out, offering a chance to flee to the remaining heroes, who stopped short as they saw the slippery mess I made of their leader. I cocked my head as they shored up, not quite running as I hoped.

Ah, well.

What had to be the second in command raised her hand and looked at the heroes gathered. Even from here, I saw the way her eyes widened, tasted the fear vibrating through her very body, the way her heart hammered in her chest.

"Stand here, stand tall! We must protect the world at all costs against Weaver. Fear not. Working together, we can take him down." She turned her attention on me, and her eyes began to glow red. Her eyes dimmed, perhaps thinking better of that, having witnessed what happened with the simpler light of the alarms. They instead began radiating darkness, blanketing the room as she snapped her fingers.

I laughed. "Clever."

The emergency lights ceased to be. But the siren still clanged on and on, filling the space between panicked shouts. I closed my eyes, welcoming the darkness. At least it was warm in the room.

"As one," she shouted again.

With my eyes shut, I saw her shout hanging in the air, commingling with the concentric waves of the siren, with the thudding footfalls of many boots headed my way. Even the smallest sound, near imperceptible, *pit-a-pat* of heartbeats made their own impression on the world around me.

"Know my name. Know fear. *Weaver.*" I released my name into that topography of sounds, echolocating each one. Using my name as a focal point, I gathered the soundwaves much as I had the light. These thrummed in my hands as I held them. The cacophony coalesced into one constant, thundering rumble. I gathered them all unto me.

Silence filled the absence left by the stolen sounds.

Like a conductor, I weaved my hands through the air. With movements much less sharp than threading light, this was more of directing the path of the sound I crafted. My hands danced as they rushed at me.

I clapped.

A shockwave echoed in front of me in a cone, loud enough to catch these supposed heroes in their tracks as a wall of all that I had drawn in and amplified rushed back at them. Pushed them back, step by step.

I advanced with it in turn.

"Weaver."

The lights flickered back on in fits and bursts, strobing erratic flashes of red as the second in command lost her grasp on darkness. I did not pause, did not hold back. The sound continued and built, with an echo of my name wafting around like a whisper from a lover.

"Weaver."

It vibrated the soft flesh of the heroes. Unrelenting. Until they collapsed and fell, blood pouring from their noses, their ears, their eyes. Their screams filled the absence left as I let the echo of my name dwindle and fade.

"They just don't make you heroes like they used to." I took another step forward, over the remnants of the first hero, and closer to the rest. These, at least, could still hear me. Maybe, depending on if shock had set in yet.

The heroine, somehow, held on and glared at me, gritting through the pain. "We...will...stop you," she spat.

I knelt and grabbed her hair. "No, I do not think you will." With a vicious twist and a violent *crack*, I left her broken on the floor.

I stood, stretching again as I did so. I turned and looked back over my shoulder at Felix, Thorn, Sabrina, and the rest.

Who all stared at me with horror. Maybe some awe.

"Are you ready to take on the world?"

Farlie, Darlie, and Tarly were the first to nod. Felix, Sabrina came next. Thorn hesitated, looking anywhere but at me, at first, before he also nodded.

With that settled, I strode to the doors, toward freedom.

The End?

EPILOGUE

Xblf wr. Dqvzhu xli hfqq.
ckgbkx ha jikseizlasvqopb mxc myw.

Afterword

Thank you for reading *The Dark Side of Super* by Matthew Siadak. Feedback from readers is both appreciated and welcomed, and reviews that are honest and from the heart will help. Leaving a review on Amazon, Goodreads, or anywhere else is very much appreciated. Many thanks for your support.

ACKNOWLEDGEMENTS

I never really thought I'd actually be writing one of these. For all of the work that I've put in, I never expected to have to write an author's acknowledgement section. Me. A published author. Here I am. I wrote a book; you're reading it. More on that in a bit.

First and foremost, I have to give thanks and acknowledge my wife and daughter. Whenever the writing bug bit, they supported me. Let me sequester myself in my office to sit down and write. My wife, who always put up with me talking about my story, and asking her what she thought, whether it was this novel or a different one. Who always let me lean on her for ideas, input, and just generally provided me all of the support I could've ever needed or wanted. Also, for this cover. Do you see how beautiful that art is? She did that. For me. I probably still owe her cookies. Let me get on that.

Second, Rho. The editor of this book, but more than that? She's the reason this book even exists. When I was having some Existential Dread™ and needed an idea to work on and had nothing, she gave me a writing prompt. From there, Felix and his power were born. A whisper on the wind to herald what was to come.

I also want to thank my brothers, who are entirely too far away from me in distance only, and who have always had my back. Thank you to my mother, and father, who helped me find a love for reading, which led me down this path of writing stories that I hope provide someone the journey they need when they need it most.

My next thanks go hand in hand with the creation of Jasper's story. My Buffalo Noodle crew, led by Bree. We did a writing jam with a communal writing prompt, and thus Jasper was born into the world, leaping right onto the stage. From Jasper, to helping me nitpick M's story, or to give me feedback on some weak points, all of them helped. I must also mention Jeremy, who has beta read two of my novels so far, and for whom I would be lost without. All of my buffaloes are the best.

From there, we're onto the Don't Make It Weird crew. If you haven't watched (or listened, if you're into aural stuff), go fix that. All of them, and the friends of the show, provided untold support for this novel, and my writing in general. Sprinting with me, sharing slipped snipplets, and Rebecca giving me some details to help flesh out Felix, and even beta reading this book. Sink pickle be praised! They are all great authors in their own right, so, maybe go check them out. You won't be sorry.

Alexis, Lawman, Molly, and the rest of the Writing Commisery peeps. Helping me to brainstorm and troubleshoot, providing that pick-me-up when I was overthinking or worrying over a piece of this story. Sprinting with me as well, cheering me on, and in general being a great group of writers to work with.

Last, and by all means, certainly not least, you. Whoever the heck you are, thank you. Whether you know me, whether we're strangers and you're giving this book a chance, however you came to find this story, thank you. Thank you for giving it, and me, a shot. Hopefully we'll cross paths again in another story somewhere down the road. May it be long and winding.

About the Author

Hailing from the St. Louis area, Matthew lives a life defined by both logic and creativity. From daylighting as a software engineer to living his true passion, writing whenever he can after the Day Job™ time is over. Whether he finds himself writing for his novels, or planning ideas with his wife for future work, or telling stories with his daughter, he loves spinning tales to entertain. On the other side of the story, he loves to tinker, to learn new things. Be it fighting with a gelatinous sourdough monster, or learning how to make vampire jam, Matthew mixes his love of creation with another passion, that of feeding people. When, or if, he finds time to sit and relax, he usually does so by playing video games, watching podcasts, or, well, finding something else to write.

Find him on most socials (Facebook, Threads, TikTok, Instagram, BlueSky) as backwardsknight, or at backwardsknight.com

Matthew Siadak,
being a goofball

Also By

www.ingramcontent.com/pod-product-compliance
Lightning Source LLC
Chambersburg PA
CBHW032312310726
48973CB00008B/2609